Transplant

David Reynolds-Moreton

sci-fi-cafe.com

Introduction

There are three stories that were written to form a loose series called The *Sapient Continuum - Transplant, Greenways* and *The Tribe* (formerly known as *The Inosculation Syndrome*). Purists would read them in that order, but Reynolds-Moreton has crafted his tales so cleverly that they can be read in any order. Fans of prequels might enjoy reading *The Tribe* first. The astute reader may even find nods to this series in his other books, of which we're proud to publish over twenty at the time of writing this introduction.

ONE:
Generation Ship

Glyn Bolstrom burst out of his nightmare into the inky blackness of the cabin, his body bathed in an ice cold sweat and shaking uncontrollably. He could still see the group of hideously distorted faces surrounding him, mouthing their obscenities as his trembling fingers groped for the elusive light sensor pad behind his head.

Wave after wave of panic surged throughout his body as he tried unsuccessfully to differentiate between reality and the terrifying sequence of events which had made up his nightmare.

Eventually, his desperately searching fingers brushed across the smooth raised surface of the sensor pad and the cabin luminary flashed into life, flooding the area around him with its harsh blue white light, adding a hint of sanity.

The grotesque collection of distorted faces slowly faded from view, but not before another shudder had rippled through his already shaking body.

Glyn breathed a sigh of relief, his breath whistling through his still chattering teeth as he heaved his body into an upright position on the bunk bed.

'I can't take much more of this.' he cried out loud.

'Having one of your nightmares again, dear?' His wife had been woken by his thrashing about as he came out of the horrible dream.

'Yes, and the damn thing is getting worse each time. I can still see their awful faces after I've put the light on. Sorry to have disturbed your sleep again.'

'Don't worry, dear. Tomorrow, or I should say today, is Sunning Day, so you can sleep on a little and catch up on your rest, there are no set tasks for you today, as far as I know. At least, I didn't see any on the screen last night.'

'Try to get back to sleep, dear, and I'll see if we can get some help in the morning.' and with that she turned over and drifted back into her slumbers.

He knew no help would be forthcoming as the Medic had broken down, or to be more precise, was only working intermittently, and then it only offered random advice which rarely fitted the problem asked of it.

Glyn would have liked to go back to sleep, but he was now afraid to in case the faces returned. One helping of that nightmare was quite enough for one sleep period, he thought.

His sleep had been disturbed for several weeks now, and the nightmare always began at the same point.

His wife was just about to give birth to their first born, although in reality they were not due to have children for some years yet, unless there was an unfortunate terminal mishap among one of the other members of the ship.

He was standing in the Medic's room at the foot of the delivery couch, and Mia was smiling sweetly at him over the huge bulge of her distended stomach.

'It won't be long now dearest, I can feel her moving about.'

At this point the door bursts open, and six birthing attendants rush into the room and spread themselves around the bed, three to each side.

They are dressed in long grey robes with cowls hiding their faces, and mutter incoherently among themselves as they lay out an assortment of surgical instruments on the edge of the couch, flashes of light mirrored from the overhead luminary unit accompanying the tinkle of steel on steel.

And then the screaming starts. At first it is just a soft low whimper, repeated again and again, and it then builds up slowly into a crescendo of sound which threatens to split his head open with its persistent screech of torment.

The attendants are jumping up and down, clapping their hands and chanting some unintelligible words which somehow seem to have some significance to him, but he can't think what it is.

Mia's face distorts into an ugly parody of what it once was, one eye sliding down to the middle of her cheek, her nose tilts sideways and creeps up the other cheek pushing the eye socket up onto her forehead. Her hair is all but gone, just a few straggly wisps of dull grey brown hang down limply, like chewed string.

Her face becomes a distorted patchwork of red and brown pimpled skin, while a dribble of dirty saliva seeps from the gaps between the few blackened and broken teeth which remain.

The attendant nearest to him pushes forward, nearly knocking him off balance, and then thrusts a gnarled and dirty hand between Mia's legs. The screaming goes a tone higher and considerably louder. Glyn's tries to shut out the torturous sounds and then the attendant braces himself against the couch and tugs and pulls strenuously, cursing and swearing.

Suddenly there is a loud 'plop' and the attendant holds a baby up by one leg, letting it swing to and fro, as if it were being blown by intermittent gusts of wind.

The cowls drop down to the attendant's shoulders, and a hideous array of faces are revealed. All are distorted and twisted to a point of being hardly recognizable as human.

One had only one eye, another, a hole where the nose should have been, the third had three eyes, one of which was in the middle of its forehead. Each had its own terrible deformity, made all the worse by their gesticulations and the high pitched ranting and raving which was going on.

One of the attendants, with putrefying sores and a piece of decaying jaw bone showing through the ruptured skin, spun around and thrust his face into Glyn's, the overpowering stench of his breath nearly making him pass out.

'Look what you've spawned, a mutant, a hideous travesty of humankind! It will have to be destroyed, burnt, mashed up into a pulp. It can't be allowed to live and breed more of its kind.' And with that he grabbed it from the other attendant and swept out of the room, the little girl child with the perfect pink skin, golden curls and pale blue eyes gurgled and smiled at Glyn, waving her chubby little hand in farewell.

Each time the nightmare occurred, it contained more detail, more sounds, and now smells were added to the deep distress Glyn had just experienced.

He dimmed the light down until it was only a gentle glow so as not to disturb his wife, and lay there, wondering what to do about the horrors of the night.

In the beginning, it hadn't been too bad, just unpleasant. Now, as the nightmare gained more detail, it was just about the most awful experience he could imagine, and the last three times it had occurred the images had remained long after he had switched on the cabin light.

He could try the Medic once more, but he couldn't remember the last time it gave out a sensible answer to a query, and no one else seemed able to help.

Glyn drifted into a half sleep state and relaxed, but not for long as the stench of the one with the putrefying sores assailed his nostrils once more and he was snap wide awake again, a new gush of ice cold sweat being added to his already wet night clothes.

As he was now fully awake, he was determined to stay that way until it was time to get up, no matter what.

'Suppose I'll get used to it in time. Anyway, it can't get any worse.' he muttered to himself. But he had thought that a few weeks ago, and it had.

To pass the time, he went over the events of the past few days, checking to see if he had done all the work assigned to him correctly, and was pleased to discover that he could find no fault with what he had done.

The lights suddenly came on fully to herald the new day, and he got up and stretched his tired body before going into the washing room for his morning rinse down.

Several others had preceded him, and among them was the team leader with whom he had discussed the nightmare problem a couple of weeks ago.

'They are getting worse, and I don't think I can take much more of it, Benz, surely there's something that can be done. It really is getting beyond a joke now.'

'Not that I know of. I'm more of a practical man, what you need is someone who is skilled with the mind, and I don't think we have anyone like that at the moment. You could try the book room, although it is only meant to represent a very tiny portion of the knowledge contained in the Teacher. Pity Teacher isn't still functioning, but it has been out of order for several generations now, so I'm told.'

'Well it's worth a try I suppose.' replied Glyn, feeling a little better as the warm air from the drying ducts caressed his body, evaporating the last few droplets of water he hadn't managed to shake off.

After completing his ablutions and dressing, he went back to his cabin and helped Mia finish tidying up before heading for the eating room where they all met up every morning to have the first meal of the day, and to find out what their duties for the next shift would be.

One of the few devices which hadn't broken down over the years was the food preparation machine. It had suffered from a few hiccups on occasions, as did the partakers of its offerings, but by and large, it had functioned in a reasonable and sane manner, at least most of the time.

Considering that it was a purely mechanical device, it managed to produce a surprisingly varied selection of menus, some of which left the consumers guessing as to what the offering was supposed to be, but generally it was good wholesome stuff, and no one had died from its culinary concoctions, as yet.

By the time Glyn and Mia had reached the eating room, everyone else had arrived and were seated, the two children and the one teenager seated with their respective parents, waiting for the day's offering to come sliding out of the hatchway.

They were greeted with nods and smiles from the assembled diners and replied in like manner, taking their places at the end of the long table.

They had barely settled into their seats when the hatch slid back with a sigh and the first two plates of today's offering appeared.

'Good God, what is it this time?' asked the recipient at the head of the table, not really expecting an answer. The two plates were passed on down the table and the next two appeared at the hatch as if by magic.

When everyone had received their portion, the comments began, most of which were humorous but some contained veiled threats as to what would have happened to the chef, had it been human.

The usual ripple of laughter accompanied the more cryptic remarks offered by the most witty of those assembled.

The food was good and wholesome and pleasant to taste, although the mechanical chef had got a little confused as to the appropriate colours for the synthetic fried egg, beans and potato fritters it had produced, but this wasn't unusual.

The meals provided by the ship were augmented by fresh fruit and vegetables gathered from the hydroponic gardens, of which there were many, the most natural of them being the current orchard with its green lawns dotted about with a selection of all the fruit bearing trees old earth had to offer at the time the ship was built.

The orchards took quite a time to come to maturity and produce their harvests, so there was a system of rotation, an old dying orchard was cleared of its trees and allowed to rest for a while, and then replanted with new stock from cuttings taken earlier.

After everyone had consumed their fill of the synthetic breakfast and a selection of fruits and berries from the side table, they all sat back engaging in light conversation, awaiting the instructions for the day to appear on the screen above the food hatchway.

As this was the seventh day of the weekly cycle, it was deemed a day of rest, and little work was required of the crew except for the inspection of the status board to ensure that all was well with the ship's equipment. Slight corrections needed could be made to bring any green lights back on, should they have changed to red, indicating a problem.

At last the screen flickered into life, and only three of the assembled diners were required to give up a little of their free time to attend the ships needs.

Glyn then told Mia about the books, and his intention to visit the book room just in case it might hold some data which could be useful in counteracting his nightmares.

'I've never been in there, what's it like?' she asked.

'I don't know, I've only heard about it. They say it's full of old books from the days of Earth, but only a token amount, as all the data we need is held by Teacher.' he replied.

'But Teacher doesn't work any more.'

'I know, that's why I'm going to the book room. No one else is able to help, so that's my only chance of finding out why I'm getting these nightmares.' He sometimes wondered if his wife was as bright as she was made out to be, but she made up for any lack of awareness by her loving care and attention to little details which made his life all the more sweet for her being there.

'I'll go along to the sunning room for a spell. Will you join me there later, dear?' she asked, smiling sweetly. 'You are looking a little pale.' she added as an afterthought.

'Yes, but I don't know when exactly. It may take a little time to find what I need from the book room, but I'll be along as soon as possible.' Glyn replied, knowing full well that he might have to miss the sunning this week if he was to find what he wanted.

The book room was not visited very often, in fact Glyn couldn't recall anyone he knew having been in there.

The main reason for this apparent lack of interest in the books was due to the fact that the room had an inert atmosphere to protect the books from the normal ravages of decay, which oxygen and moisture in normal air would produce.

This meant wearing a suit complete with air supply if one wanted to study the works of the ancients, and not many were prepared to put up with the extra hassle of so doing.

Teacher had broken down some three generations ago, but as the youngsters were taught all that the adults knew, including reading and writing, there was little need for the book room. It was just a museum, a small token of that which was, a reminder of how things were done in a bygone age, but which could now prove its worth.

Not being sure where the book room was, Glyn headed for the equipment room where all the necessary tools and materials for repairs were issued when something wore out or needed a little attention. He remembered that a map of the ship's layout was on one wall, and the book room should be on it.

The ship was big, very big, and it was some time later when he entered the equipment room, much to the surprise of its occupants. 'What are you doing here, Glyn? I didn't think you were called to duty today,' said one of the men, loading tools into a carry bag.

'I'm trying to find the book room, it should be somewhere on the wall map of the ship.' Glyn replied, trying to make the answer as nonchalant as possible, thus avoiding a possible long explanation of his need to find the room.

Luckily they took no notice of his answer, and carried on loading their tools while Glyn scanned the wall map for the elusive book repository.

At last he found it, tucked away in a corner of the main map, and perhaps a good twenty minutes walk away from his present position.

Making a mental note of its relationship to one of the hydroponics gardens he knew well, Glyn turned and bade farewell to the tool collectors with a wave of his hand, and set off down the corridor in what he thought was the correct direction.

Striding off purposefully on his quest, he wondered what a book looked like, and how he would know which one contained the necessary information. Glyn could read and write proficiently, as all members of the ship could, but he had only seen written reports and messages so far, and wondered if a book was like a report, but bigger.

He was a little out of breath as he passed the hydroponics chamber where the passageway split into four, and slowed his pace to make sure of his bearings. The map had shown that the book room was off a small corridor which in turn was off the main one he was now in, but this was new territory to him and he felt a little uneasy as he walked on into the unknown regions of the ship.

As he marched on, he noticed several light tubes in the ceiling of the corridor had burnt out, and no one had bothered to replace them. This could only mean that very few, if any, had been to the book room, or even down this corridor, for a long time.

A feeling of loneliness overcame Glyn as he hurried on, and he felt even more uneasy as he reached the turn off for the book room. This corridor clearly hadn't been trodden for some time, as a layer of dust had collected on the floor showing his footprints up as he looked back. The normal dust removal system must have broken down, and no one had noticed. As this wasn't a vital function of the ship, he supposed the maintenance computer had ignored the fault, leaving it to the humans to repair, if they didn't like dust.

Most doors had numbers on them, while some had numbers and their purpose spelt out in letters. Glyn hoped that the book room was one of the latter, as he didn't know the number of the room and hadn't thought to find it out before he began his journey.

Checking each door as he went, he began to wonder if he had passed the room, as the corridor seemed never ending and the only markings on the doors were in numbers.

A feeling of panic hit hard as he realized that he was cut off from the rest of the ship's members by a great distance, and if he got lost who would be able to find him?

He found some relief in the knowledge that the tool collectors knew where he was going, and if the worst came to the worst, and he was missed, they would no doubt set up a search party.

Feeling a little brighter at the thought of possible rescue, he almost passed the door of the book room in the gloom from a failed lamp.

The door was clearly marked 235 with BOOK ROOM printed beneath the number. Glyn pressed the usual button in the centre of the door and it obligingly hissed open, revealing a small and cramped chamber beyond.

He entered the chamber, the door hissed closed behind him, and the old feeling of fear returned. He shook it off, looking around for the air suit he knew he would have to wear in order to enter the actual book room.

It hung on a peg high up on the wall, a long flexible tube protruding from the back section which then snaked around and disappeared into a socket on the wall.

As Glyn struggled into the suit, he wondered how they had decided what size to make it, and found the designers had indeed been generous in their specifications, as it hung on him like a lose fitting bag and would therefore fit anyone, if fit was the right word.

The head gear was a cumbersome thing to have to contend with, and he could well see this was yet another reason why this room wasn't the most popular one on the ship.

Clamping the helmet into place, he took a couple of steps towards the entrance door of the room, and was pulled up short by the air hose.

Realizing that he would have to disconnect it, he did so, instinctively holding his breath.

The inner door opened to reveal an odd shaped room, the walls lined with what he thought were the books, with a dim light over a table in the middle. Just inside the door was a socket for the air hose, and he reconnected it hurriedly, gasping in a breath of fresh air.

The shape of the room wasn't the normal square or oblong enclosure he was used to, but more reminiscent of the space when several odd shaped rooms were brought together, and the book room was that left over space where they joined.

He went over to the nearest wall and slowly pulled a book from the shelf where it had rested for several hundred years. Fearful that it might disintegrate, he gently laid it down on the table and opened the cover.

'A Collection of British Butterflies' adorned the top of the first page, and beneath it was a picture of a butterfly with spread open wings, a glorious golden thing.

Having never seen one before, Glyn didn't know what a butterfly actually was, but he was able to identify it as a member of the insect family as he had seen insects in the hydroponics gardens, but none as beautiful as this.

A strange lump came up in his throat, and all thoughts of his purpose for being there fled as he slowly turned over the pages, drinking in the sheer beauty of the illustrations and wishing these creatures were needed to pollinate the gardens on the ship.

It took a while to go through to the end, and with a sigh he reluctantly replaced it on the shelf, and set about trying to find how he could identify the book he had come for.

Set in the wall between the books was an oblong panel, with the word INDEX at its top. There didn't appear to be any controls to work the index, no buttons or switches that he could see, so he laid his hand on the main panel to see if it would respond to his presence. There was a slight flicker of light, a hint of some lettering, and then it went blank and stayed that way, despite repeated touches and not a few thumps from a very frustrated Glyn.

He gave up fiddling with the inoperative index after a while, and returned to the shelves of books, which he found to his amazement were in no special order that he could discern. They certainly were not filed by author or subject, and he supposed that over the years they had been put back in a random fashion by those who had used them.

Selecting another book at random, he sat at the table and opened it. It appeared to be a condensed history of earth from the time of the Romans, who ever they were, up to the time of the smelting stations which had encircled earth. It seemed that raw materials were in very short supply, and the asteroid belt was being mined for anything useable in the way of minerals.

The end of the book seemed to be contemporary with the period in which the Great Ship had been built, although there had been no mention of it that Glyn could find.

He had only a scant knowledge of the history of the Great Ship, as it was referred to, and that was on a 'hand me down' basis from his forebears. His interest in the ship had been reawakened by the book, and he decided to find out as much about it as possible, but first he must locate the necessary data to stop the awful nightmares.

Several random selections provided a mine of interesting things to study, but so far there was nothing about dreams.

It was only when he began to feel hungry that he was aware of how long he had spent in the company of the books, and checking his time piece he realized that he would have to hurry if he was to get to the eating room before it was too late for the midday meal, and a panic ensued at his absence.

The journey back to a familiar area of the ship took less time than he expected, and he began to wonder if he had accidentally taken a short cut, but later when he consulted the map of the area, he knew he hadn't, he'd just been very hungry and in a hurry.

During the meal Glyn explained to Mia what he had been doing, but although she listened intently, and asked the right questions, she showed little interest in joining him in his quest for knowledge.

He now had a new interest in life, and impatiently waited for the rest of the ship's members to finish eating so that he could get back to the books.

The bowl of fruit had just been passed around the table, when the screen above the food hatch lit up, a gong sounded and the voice of the Captain echoed across the eating room, his words printed out on the screen as he spoke.

'There has been a malfunction in hydroponics garden number H233, please attend at once and correct.'

The Captain had never been seen, and rarely spoke except in an emergency, so everyone took what he had to say very seriously. It was rumoured that he was just an extension of the vast computer system which ran the ship, but no one was sure.

For a moment Glyn forgot about his books as he and three others volunteered for the duty call, and went immediately to the equipment room to collect whatever the ship deemed necessary for the operation.

'Looks like we'll have to suit up.' one of them said as four bright yellow anti-contamination suits spilled out onto the floor from a locker.

'Something must have gone horribly wrong for us to have to wear suits.' Glyn added, a feeling of dread welling up from his stomach.

There had been a spate of mishaps in the hydroponics department of late, and the worrying events seemed to becoming more frequent.

'Better check the route for the shortest possible journey, as this is one I don't know.' one of the team said, looking up at the spider web like corridor map on the wall.

'It's down three levels and off to one side of where we are now, and that's quite a distance. You'd think they would have put in some form of simple transport, wouldn't you?'

'At least it gives us some exercise,' Glyn said, 'and one or two of us could well do with it.' he added, with a glancing grin at one of the team who was a little over weight.

Just then there was a loud thump as a purple canister with a white skull and crossbones on it came out of a chute and rolled across the floor of the equipment room.

'This must be serious, I've never seen one of these before,' Glyn said to no one in particular, 'and what do we do with it? There are no instructions on it as far as I can see.'

'I don't like the sound of this event. I thought the Captain's voice was a little strained when he spoke to us earlier, so maybe this is a major catastrophe.' one of the team said.

'Oh, come on, the Captain is only a computer voice, it can't show any emotion like we can.' Glyn felt sad that any of them should be so naive as to give credence to the story of the Captain being human and aloof from them all, hidden away in a little place of his own.

'Well, it's never been proved one way or the other, and I think there may well be something to it. After all, most things have broken down or developed a fault at some time, but the Captain never has, so perhaps he is real after all.'

'Come on you two, we'll sort this out later on if you really must, but drop it for now and let's get on with the problem of the hydroponics cell.'

The four of them staggered out of the room laden with an assortment of equipment that should fix just about anything, or so they thought.

Clanking and rattling their way along the corridor, they came to the first of the lifts they would have to use. It was a tight squeeze to get all four of them in, and the equipment, but they made it, just.

The lift was silent in its movement, and they only knew they had reached the lower level when the door hissed open to reveal a service tunnel.

'I thought we were using the normal corridors.' said Glyn.

'So did I,' Brendon added, 'but it looks as if there is something wrong with the corridor we want or the lift doesn't know what it's doing.'

'Let's go back up and try coming down again, that should prove the point.' Glyn suggested.

One of the team shuffled round, found the correct button and they returned to the corridor they had started from.

'Right, now let's see what happens.' and the lift descended once more to stop at the service tunnel.

'I didn't know such tunnels existed.' commented one member of the team.

'I've never seen one, although I did hear about them some time ago,' added Brendon, grumpily 'and I don't like the idea of going in. We would have to bend up double and with all this equipment, I don't think we could make it.'

Glyn poked his head cautiously into the tunnel and looked up and down it. The light level was very low and it had a dry dusty smell about it, and then he spotted a very good reason for not entering.

'It looks as if there are two rails sunk into the floor and that can only mean that something on wheels goes along it. If we are in the tunnel when whatever it is comes along......' He didn't need to finish the sentence.

'Looks like we shall have to try and find another connection to the corridor we want, but is it above us or below?' Arki, the tall one asked.

'Damned if I know. Perhaps we should go back up again, go along the corridor and try another lift.' Brendon offered.

'Good idea.' replied Glyn, and they all wriggled round so that one of them could reach the control button, their equipment making a cacophony of clanks and rattles in the confined space of the lift, and up they went.

The next lift was some way along the seemingly never ending maze of passageways in the Great Ship, and it was a disgruntled bunch of men who eventually piled into the box like space which had been designed for two in comfort, and three at a squeeze.

'Let's hope this one works correctly.' said Glyn, thumbing the button a little more firmly than was necessary.

The lift dropped to the required level as far as they could tell, and when they emerged into the lower corridor, the number sequence on the doors corresponded with those they'd seen on the ship's map back in the equipment room.

'We shall have to go back up that way,' indicated Glyn, 'until we come to an intersection, and then turn off to the left.'

'No, to the right.' Arki said, but with little certainty.

'I've got a bit of paper here somewhere, let's draw out the route you memorized from the wall map, and then we can put in the diversion we've just made.' Brendon said, looking at Arki.

Although they referred to it as paper, it was really a thin sheet of plastic material on which they could write, and then wipe off the writing in order to use the sheet again. Old names for commodities still stuck long after the materials from which they were made had been replaced with something else.

Arki drew out the map, made the corrections for the diversion, and apologized for his mistake.

'One day someone is going to get lost in this labyrinth.' he added, still not happy that he had made a mistake which could have caused even more problems for the group.

'Never happened yet, as far as I know.' Glyn added, trying to add a note of cheer to the proceedings.

They trudged on, coming at last to the door marked H223 and paused before it, putting down their equipment.

'Better suit up, we can't go in there without protection as there is a flashing red light on the door.' Brendon commented, sourly.

'How do you know that?' asked Arki, still smarting from his mistake.

'Don't know really, must have heard it somewhere, anyway that light isn't there just to make the door look pretty, it's a warning.'

They struggled into their protection suits, locked the head pieces into place and checked their radio communications units. All seemed well.

'OK, let's do it.' said Glyn, who seemed to have assumed leadership by default.

He pressed the pad to activate the door's opening mechanism, and after a pause it obligingly slid to one side. The four of them crowded into the small space of the airlock, the outer door slid to and a green light came on to indicate that they could proceed into the problematic hydroponics chamber.

The chamber was vast, stretching upwards into a mist shrouded ceiling which they assumed was there, but couldn't see. A long wide walkway stretched off into the distance, each side of it shrouded in banks of deep green foliage, some of which had decayed and drooped downwards to block the centre path in places, a general mistiness hung in the air adding to the sense of gloom.

'What are we supposed to do?' asked Brendon, looking around nervously as if expecting something nasty to come out of the foliage at them. They put their equipment down and looked around at the vast green jungle.

Glyn was just about to ask the same question when the 'ping' which heralded the voice of the Captain sounded, but with a strangely muffled sound to it.

'Please look around you and tell what you see. The optics in this unit have malfunctioned and I am unable to observe the situation.'

They all looked at one another in astonishment, the captain didn't usually ask questions or require their help, he, if it was a 'he', just gave orders and made announcements.

The other three looked at Glyn, Brendon raising his hands and shrugging his shoulders. Glyn realized that they had unanimously chosen him to be their spokesman on the subject of the chamber without saying a word.

He quickly looked around the vast cavern of greenery to make sure he hadn't missed anything important, and said,

'This end of the chamber is nearly normal, as far as I can see, with only a few clumps of leaves showing signs of decay, but further on down the line I can see whole branches laden with a dirty green brown mess of decayed vegetation, some of it has actually turned into a liquid and is dripping off the ends of the branches. Good thing we can't smell it.

'There is a blockage further on down the chamber, I will try to get past it so that I can see what the rest of the chamber looks like.' He walked up to the first branch which had bent right down to ground level, the slime from the dripping end forming a small pool of disgusting bubbling liquid which he was very careful not to tread in or get on his suit.

Glyn went to push the blocking branch to one side, and as his hand touched it there was a soggy snapping sound and it fell to the ground, a thin drizzle of brown liquid oozing out of the broken end which was still attached to the main growth. The piece which had fallen split open along its length, adding more of the putrefying liquid to the slime pool in the middle of the path.

He bent as close to the ruptured branch as his stomach would allow to see if there were any signs of living creatures in the remains which might have caused the disintegration, but nothing moved except the turgid liquid still oozing out of the collapsed branch.

Carefully he stepped over the nauseous looking mess on the path and slowly walked on down between the towering ranks of plants, most of which showed signs of succumbing to the rot in varying degrees.

Brendon had followed him a few paces down the track way and was getting nervous, calling over the radio link

'You are disappearing into the mist, I can only just make out your shape. Do you think it wise to be out of sight?'

Glyn hesitated for a moment, he didn't like the idea of being out of sight just in case something went wrong, and no one knew about it.

'OK, as the mist begins to hide me, come forward, keeping me just in sight, and then the others can do likewise as you begin to fade from sight. That way we shall all know what's going on and can render help if necessary.'

Slowly Glyn edged his way past fallen branches and pools of slime, which were becoming more numerous as he proceeded down the pathway between the towering plant growth.

'What do you see now?' the voice of the Captain sounded uneasy, but Glyn put it down to his imagination as he felt sure the Captain wasn't really human.

'More of the same, except that it is getting worse, every plant is affected to some degree, some have collapsed completely.'

A few minutes later and the foursome had gone as far as they could, spread out along the pathway and keeping each other just in sight.

Glyn had reached a point where he thought he could see the end of the chamber wall in the now very steamy conditions, and called back on the radio that he wasn't going any further as his way was blocked by too many fallen branches.

Again the attention getting 'ping' sounded, to be followed by the sonorous tones of the Captain.

'Take the purple canister up to the end of the chamber, pull the tab on the top, the end will come off. This reveals a valve. Hold the canister vertically, turn the valve until the arrow points to the mark and then raise it up as high as you can. Turn to face the way back to the entrance port. Press the button next to the valve and walk back to the port.'

As the canister in question was back at the point where they had all come in, there were a few muttered curses as the foursome trouped back to recover it.

When the little group had reassembled at the pile of equipment they had dumped earlier, it was the fourth member of the team, Bolin, who volunteered to activate the canister which brought an audible sigh of relief from the other three.

This time they set off as a group to the far end of the chamber, helping each other over fallen branches and taking it in turns to carry the heavy canister.

As they made their way back to the far end of the chamber, Glyn gave the Captain a running commentary of their progress and the degree of increasing decay they observed as they went down the pathway, hoping the information would be of some use.

When they had gone as far as it was deemed safe to go and with what they thought was the end of the chamber in sight, they halted, informed the Captain that they were about to release whatever it was the canister held, and prepared to walk back the way they had come.

Bolin removed the end of the canister as instructed, turned the valve and held the canister as high as he could.

'Someone else will have to press the release button, I can't reach it and hold this damn thing at the same time.'

Brendon stepped forward a couple of paces, thought better of it, and stayed put.

'OK, I'll do it.' said Glyn stepping up to the nervous looking Bolin. He pressed the button and stepped back in one fluid movement, as if expecting the canister to come alive. All that happened was a faint hissing sound and an almost invisible stream of vapour jetting high up into the air.

'Looks harmless enough, but I wouldn't count on it.' Glyn felt something should be said, if only to ease the tension they all felt.

Slowly they made their way back towards the entrance point of the chamber, helping Bolin with his canister wherever a branch got in the way or a pool of slime had to be trodden in, as the fluid from the decaying vegetation dripped down from the rotting branches at an ever increasing rate.

Glyn kept the Captain informed of their progress as they went along until they neared the end of the pathway by the entrance, and then disaster struck.

A large branch fell from high above, knocking Bolin off his feet and sending the canister spinning into the slimy mass of decay at the side of the path. As he fell his arm caught on one of the steel posts which marked the edge of the path, ripping the suit open and exposing bare flesh.

As the others crowded around him, a thin trickle of blood appeared and a look of horror flashed across Bolin's face.

Glyn quickly told the Captain what had happened, but there was no reply for a moment.

'Come on Captain, what do we do now? Bolin's been injured, what should we do?'

'Recover the canister and go to the end of the chamber. It is vital that the operation be completed. Do it now.'

'But what about Bolin?'

'Recover the canister....' the Captain just repeated his former order.

Arki squelched his way into the morass at the side of the path, recovered the canister, and holding it as high as he could walked on up the path, cursing under his breath.

Bolin was looking decidedly sick inside his face mask, his skin had taken on a pale grey colour and he was trembling.

'Bolin, can you hear me? Stand up, come on, stand up.' but Glyn was wasting his breath, Bolin slowly slipped into unconsciousness and slithered from their grasp to lie on the pathway in a crumpled heap.

'Is he dead?' asked an equally pale Brendon.

'No, I don't think so, but he's very sick. We must try and get him back to our quarters as quickly as possible, someone may know what to do.' although in all honesty, Glyn didn't think anyone would.

'Captain, what can we do for Bolin?' asked Arki, returning to the group and not really expecting a reply.

'What has happened to him?' came back loud and clear.

'He fell against a steel post and gashed his suit, he also cut his arm on it and now he's unconscious, what should we do?' Arki was getting irritated at having to repeat himself.

'There is nothing anyone can do for him. The spray from the canister must have got into his blood stream. He will die very soon and his body will disintegrate. Please place his body on the side of the pathway and it will be disposed of along with the vegetation.'

They looked at one another in sheer disbelief that the Captain could be so callous and uncaring towards one of them, it was his duty to look after them, or so they thought.

'We can't just leave him here.' Brendon said, his voice sounding lumpy and strained over the radio link.

'It looks as if we shall have to. We don't know what's wrong with him, and I doubt if anyone else does. If the spray has killed him, and that's what the Captain implied, then he will be carrying whatever it is in his body, and that could then spread to the rest of us if we take him out of his suit.'

Glyn was having trouble making his voice sound level and normal due to the lump in his throat.

Arki lifted the unfortunate man's arm to look at the wound, and a thin stream of brown fluid poured out causing him to drop it and jump back quickly.

'Whatever that stuff is, it certainly works quickly.' he said, and then they looked at the forest of vegetation down through the length of the huge chamber.

It had crumbled into a limp mass of soggy twisted branches with hardly a leaf in sight, both sides of the pathway seemed to be alive as the few remaining weakened branches bent under their own weight, wriggling and twisting against each other as they slumped downwards to join the writhing mass of slush on the floor of the chamber.

'I think we had better get out of here as soon as possible, we've done our job, at some cost, so I'll check with the Captain to see if we can go.' Glyn said, but before anyone could agree or otherwise, the Captain's voice boomed back,

'You must all leave the chamber now and go to the decontamination room, I will direct you there. This chamber will be flushed out as soon as the last few branches have been turned into liquid form, and you would not be able to survive that.'

Bolin's head was lying at an awkward angle and Arki bent to straighten it out, at least it would look better, he thought. As he lifted the head, several litres of brown fluid poured out of the split in the arm rent and all three nearly lost the remains of their breakfast.

That was enough, and they struggled to pick up their equipment along with Bolin's, and headed for the exit as quickly as was decently possible.

'Please enter the lift. You will be taken to a decontamination point.

Please make sure you have all your issued equipment with you, nothing must be left behind.'

'What about Bolin?' asked Brendon.

'There is nothing we can do for Bolin, as the Captain said. He is dead. And now his body will be returned to the recycling unit.'

'I can't see the Captain going in there to fish his body out, so that must mean that everything in there will be turned into a liquid and then recycled. I don't like the sound of that somehow.'

'It's normal procedure Arki, if you think about it. All our unwanted materials go to the recycling unit, including us, if the truth were known.' said Glyn, trying to add a note of calm to the situation.

'When people die, they go to the room of rest.' Brendon interjected, a nervous tone to his voice as if a long held myth was about to be exposed for what it was.

'Of course they do,' Glyn replied, 'but where do you think they go after that? Everything has to be recycled, or there wouldn't be anything left after a few years.'

They all really knew what happened, it was just that some didn't want to think about it in any detail.

The lift door obligingly opened at their approach and they all crowded in, the door hissed to and Glyn automatically shuffled around to reach the control buttons.

'I don't see anything marked decontamination, so what do we do now?' he asked.

'You will be taken to decontamination.' The voice of the Captain boomed in the confined space of the lift cubicle. 'It is completely automatic.' And the lift began to move.

The door opened into a larger cubicle into which they all trooped, glad of a bit more space to move around in.

'What happens to us now?' whimpered Brendon, looking around anxiously at a cage like structure against the far wall.

'Be patient, the Captain will tell us.' replied Glyn, placing a hand on Brendon's shoulder, which made him jump.

'Please enter the cage in front of you. Place your equipment evenly over the floor of the cage. You will be submerged in a decontamination fluid. It is quite safe. You have your own air supply contained within the structure of your suits. When the fluid is over your heads, please rotate on the spot, raising your arms above your head.' The command level of the Captain's voice had gone up a couple of notches, and they all trooped obediently forward, doing as instructed.

The cage door slid to behind them with a clank, and a sudden jerk indicated that they were on their way down into the darkness below.

As the cage descended, a milky white fluid surged up around their feet, foaming as it raced around any obstacles in its path. Brendon had now gone a very pale shade of grey as the light disappeared to be replaced with the seething decontamination fluid.

As it closed over their heads they could feel the fluid being pulsed in a series of powerful jets pushing against their bodies, making it difficult to retain their positions without bumping into each other in the confined space.

Raising their arms above their heads and rotating as instructed, proved even more difficult as their feet kept tripping over the equipment on the floor of the cage.

Without warning the fluid level dropped, light returned and they stood looking at each other, their vision distorted by the milky fluid still clinging to their face plates.

'Thank goodness that's over.' Glyn said over his radio link, but no sooner had the words been uttered when a fresh surge of clear fluid foamed up around their feet, and they were soon submerged again.

The pulsing jets began again, and they obediently raised their arms and rotated. Glyn wondered what they must have looked like to an observer, concluding that the word must have been ridiculous.

When the pulsing stopped, it was replaced by a low frequency vibration which seemed to penetrate their very bodies, making them feel sick, and that caused a considerable amount of concern as they could well choke within the confines of their helmets.

The fluid drained away again, the cage rose up to the level above and the door slid back, inviting them to leave the cage, not that any encouragement was really needed.

Somewhere a fan started up, the whine of the blades rising to a crescendo as a blast of hot air buffeted them about, and they rotated once more with their arms vertical.

When whatever it was had decided they were sufficiently dry, the fan was cut off and all was quiet again.

'When the tone sounds, please close your eyes tightly. Do not look at the light source, it will damage your retinas beyond repair.' In a way, it was comforting to hear the voice of the Captain again, Glyn thought.

The 'ping' sounded, and they screwed their eyes as tightly shut as it was humanly possible to do as a searing blast of blue white light hit them with what seemed like almost physical force.

The light switched off, and they were left in what seemed to be total darkness, but slowly their vision returned and a sigh of relief echoed around the radio links.

'You are now decontaminated. Please return your apparatus to the equipment room. Your exit from this room is opposite to that which you entered from. You will be guided back to your quarters.'

'Thank you for your co-operation, that is all.' The faintest of clicks indicated that the Captain was no longer on line, and they were alone in the bowls of the great ship.

'I hope the device which gives directions hasn't broken down,' Arki offered, 'or we shall be in real trouble.' Before anyone could answer the door slid open to reveal a dark passage ahead, and they hesitatingly moved forward thinking over what Arki had said.

The door of the decontamination room slid to behind them with a definite click, and they knew there was no way back in as there were no controls on what now looked like a normal passage wall, and there was no sign of where the doorway had been.

The corridor ran to left and right, the left section being more brightly lit, so they headed along it, hoping they were doing the right thing.

They had been walking for some minutes when a section of the corridor wall slid back, and they all stopped.

'I suppose we are intended to go in,' Glyn commented, 'I don't go much on the 'directions' we are supposed to receive.'

There was nowhere else to go as the lights up ahead in the corridor had dimmed, the lift now offering the only fully lighted area.

This time they felt the surge as the lift went upwards, stopped, moved sideways, changed directions several times and then went up again.

When the door opened into a now familiar section of the ship, they were totally confused as to where they had been, and feeling not a little dizzy.

'Thank goodness we're back in one piece, I really didn't think we'd make it.' Brendon said, smiling for the first time since breakfast. Glyn gave him a pat on the back and said,

'We'd better report back to the others and tell them what's happened to Bolin. Let's dump the equipment and then it will almost be time for the next meal, so we can tell them then.' Without realizing it, Glyn had taken full control over the little group, and they had accepted it quite naturally.

After laying out their equipment on the long bench like shelf along one wall of the equipment room, they left it for the machinery to check over and store in the appropriate sections for reuse at a later date.

A few diners had arrived when the trio trooped in, and Glyn said that it would be best to wait for all to assemble before relating what had happened, and the others agreed.

Slowly the room filled up with the other members of the ship, and when all were seated Glyn stood up to make his announcement.

'I have some sad news for you all. Bolin is no longer with us. He had an accident down in the hydroponics chamber, and there was nothing we could do to help him, even the Captain couldn't help. I won't go into the unpleasant details of what happened, but he is no more, and as far as we can tell, didn't suffer much. He will be missed by us all, I'm sure, and as we can't say farewell to him in the normal manner, I suggest we hold a one minute silence, and think about him.'

After the look of shock had passed, they bowed their heads and a minute of silence began, extending into several minutes as no one wanted to be the first to break what little respect they could pay to a much loved member of the ship.

Most of the meal was eaten in silence, and it wasn't until after the fruit bowl had been passed around did any real conversation take place, and then it was only of a trivial nature. It was a rare thing to lose someone accidentally.

Fortunately no one asked Glyn for details of what happened to Bolin, and he was glad, as he didn't want to go through the horror of the incident again.

As the meal time break ended and the diners departed to go their various ways, Mia turned towards Glyn and asked him, 'Will you be going to the sunning room, dear? You missed your session this morning.'

'No I don't think so, I'd rather go to the book room, there's something I want to find out and it may be in one of the books.' He replied, not that he had anything specific in mind, but he wanted to be alone for a while, there were things to think about and he didn't want any interruptions. She just nodded and smiled. He sometimes wished she would show a little more interest in life, a little more spark.

The first time he had gone to the book room he had some difficulty in finding it, but this time he suddenly found himself there, not being aware of the journey apart from the last few metres.

The fact that he had to suit up again didn't seem to matter this time, and he went into the main room and sat down. Just what was it he wanted to find out? He wasn't sure, but he felt it had something to do with the Captain, but what? He felt quite sure that the Captain was just an extension of the computer system which ran the ship, similar in a way to Teacher and Medic before they had ceased to function.

He began a random selection of the books, one here, one there, finding the contents of most of them interesting, but nothing really grabbed his attention.

A systematic search was the only way he was going to find what he thought he wanted, and so he pulled the chair over to the narrow end of the room, climbed up, and began checking each book in turn.

There was a lot of information here he thought, but virtually nothing pertinent to the ship or how it was run. It was when he reached the last book on the top shelf that he came upon the first clue in his search.

The title on the spine 'Cement manufacture in the twentieth century' seemed an odd selection for a book representative of Earth's history, so he pulled it out to take a quick look at its contents.

A small clasp held the book closed, and he returned to the table to try and release it. Why should a book, which was intended to be read, have a clasp to seal its contents? He felt his heart beat a little faster, surely this couldn't be just another ordinary book, and he fiddled with the clasp until it suddenly sprang open, and the contents were exposed.

He had been right, this was no ordinary book, but one made up from separate sheets laced together and placed in the cover of a book whose contents had been removed.

It was hand written in a clear script which made easy reading, and he dragged the chair back to the table, sat down and almost reverently turned the first page.

> 'My name is Jon Silworth, I am twenty four years old, and of the third generation on board this great ship which is into its one hundred and twelfth year in its mission to find mankind a new home among the stars.
>
> According to the Teacher, which is a computer driven device intended to educate the new born, the ship was built by a consortium of very wealthy and philanthropic individuals who foresaw the demise of mankind on planet Earth.
>
> The main reason for writing this record of our lives here is so

that if anything should go wrong with the system, then those who are to come will have a record of things as we have seen them, and the purpose of this great venture.

The ship is vast, but we do not know of its true size as we only have access to certain parts of it. Everything is recycled automatically, so sustaining our needs. Most things seem to be self repairing, as far as we can tell, only occasionally do we have to physically replace or repair items as instructed by the Captain, whom we have never seen, but assume is part of the crew in a separate section of the ship. Why they are apart from us, we do not know, but there must be a reason. Perhaps we shall meet when we find our new home.

There is one aspect of our life which some of us do not agree with, and that is the allocation of mating partners and the production of the next generation.

Our numbers are strictly controlled, and that is reasonable, or the ship would not be able to sustain our needs, but the choosing of partners is something we would like to do ourselves. When this was queried with Teacher, we were informed that only the Medic could make an accurate selection of mates to ensure the correct mixing of genes.

While I can see the sense of this, there are a few dissenters in this generation who, for some reason unknown to me, cannot understand this need, and have gone to great lengths to try to override the system. So far, they have been unsuccessful due to the clever way in which the system has been set up.

Although some couples have tried to mate of their own choosing and conceive children thereby, they have been unable to produce any offspring. Only couples selected by the Medic can conceive, and then only when instructed to do so. The chosen couple are requested to visit the Medic's room where something takes place, but we do not know what it is or how it is done, and then a child is born to them after the appropriate time.

The sex of the child is predetermined in some way to suit the needs of the project, and this sometimes causes dissent among those who want a child of the other sex. Fortunately, there seems to be nothing they can do to outwit the will of the 'ship', as they see it. The other matter of concern to some of us, but not me, is the way in which the bodies of those who die are disposed of.

They are taken to a little room where the last farewells are said, and then the body which has been placed on a table like structure disappears into a hole in the wall, to be broken down and its materials recycled somehow.

A small quasi religious body, luckily with few members, object to the recycling system, and are in constant argument with Teacher about it, but to no avail. I do not understand their reasoning, and I suspect there is none that will stand up to close scrutiny.

It is said that it takes all sorts to make a world, and that rule seems to apply here on our little world!

Yesterday there was a commotion in one of the hydroponics chambers, but I only heard about it. A team of three were gathering fruit when it was discovered that one tree had produced several fruits which were twice the size we were used to, and they had a somewhat distorted shape.

When this was commented on the Captain must have overheard it, and ordered the fruit and the tree to be destroyed, or I should say recycled.

One of the team objected, saying that he thought it was a good idea to keep the extra large fruit and even breed new trees from it. This did not go down well with the Captain, who then reinstated his earlier orders and threatened to destroy the whole chamber of trees if they did not comply at once.

When I heard about it I asked Teacher why the Captain had acted this way, and Teacher said it was important to keep every growing thing pure in a genetic sense, as no one knew what effect a mutated life form would have on us if we consumed it. It makes sense to me, but I wonder why the Captain did not explain it at the time.

I have often thought it strange that we still use the old Earth time, hours, days, weeks and years, when we have the chance to make a new and more rational time marking system.

Teacher said it was to give us a feeling of continuity with the past, I suppose it's right.

We are kept busy most of the time, doing things which I sometimes suspect are not really necessary. There is a machine shop where those who have been taught the necessary skills are called upon to manufacture spare parts for the ship, but I sometimes wonder if this is only a means of keeping us occupied, as I am sure the ship could make anything it requires.

Glyn read on, each page revealing a little more about the attitudes of the ship's members at that time towards the project and their hopes and aspirations for the future.

Realizing that he had spent a little more time in the book room than he had intended, he carefully noted the page number he had reached and replaced the diary on the end of the top shelf where he had found it, resolving to return at the next possible opportunity.

Returning to his cabin, he found Mia in a state of great excitement.

'Arki has worked it out that we are the most likely couple to be allowed to have a child, now that Bolin has gone, what do you think of that?'

'I'm delighted of course, but it seems a pity that we had to lose Bolin in order for this to happen.'

'But we would have to lose somebody before I could conceive, so what does it matter?'

'Looked at like that, I don't suppose it does matter, it was just the way we lost him that hurts.'

Glyn decided to let the matter drop, as in his opinion, Mia's view of things always seemed a little superficial to him, and it wasn't worth the trouble to try and explain how he felt.

He changed the subject by trying to interest Mia in his discovery in the book room, but she showed little more than polite interest, so the conversation died as it usually did on matters other than the more mundane happenings on board the ship.

Mia wouldn't have been his natural choice for a mate, but as they had been allotted to each other on the basis of the correct mixing of genes with regard to their offspring, he accepted the inevitable, but he would have preferred someone with a little more spark and curiosity. Apart from that one fault, as he saw it, she was the perfect companion, and always ready to support and comfort him when needed.

It was time for their evening meal break, and Glyn and Mia joined the others as they gathered in the eating room, chatting lightly among themselves, although the topic of Bolin's misfortune was noticeably absent.

The food appeared as always, the usual comments accompanying each dish as it slid through the hatchway, but somehow the sting had gone out of the ribald remarks reserved for the culinary delights of the mechanical chef. Bolin's demise was having a far greater effect than was apparent on the surface of things.

By the time the fruit and berry stage of the meal had been reached, the conversation had dwindled to the occasional acknowledgement as the fruit bowl was passed around and the odd muttered curse as someone bit into the stone at the heart of the fruit they were eating, their attention not being fully on what they were doing. Bolin was going to be missed by many for some time to come.

The usual soft 'ping' heralding an announcement from the Captain took everyone's attention, and all turned towards the screen above the hatchway where the spoken words would also be displayed for all to read. There was little chance of a verbal being misinterpreted that way.

'After the meal break, Glyn and Mia will go to the Medic's room. It has been decided that the time is right for you to have a child. I offer my congratulations and good wishes for the happy event which is to follow.'

A light round of applause followed the announcement, and all turned towards the lucky couple, smiling and nodding their heads in agreement.

Glyn, always keen to acquire extra data, saw a chance to get a little more information out of the Captain and said,

'I thought the Medic had fallen from his highly exalted perch and was only offering random wisdom these days, so is it safe for us to put ourselves into his somewhat befuddled hands?'

'It is quite safe. The Medic's verbal and screen abilities have malfunctioned but the equipment is operating correctly. You have nothing to fear.'

'Can we not repair the Medic? its help is often needed.'

'It is beyond the capabilities of those present to achieve this. I have taken over the duties of the Medic and will issue medical instructions when required.'

'Can you not repair the Medic? Or could we not do so under your instruction?'

'That is not possible, I am sorry.'

'What will happen to us if your circuits break down?' Glyn was taking a chance with such a barbed question, but he was into his stride now and cared little for the consequences of such an impertinent query.

The ensuing silence was almost deafening, and everyone glanced to and fro from Glyn to the screen, hardly believing what they had just heard.

The softest of clicks indicated that the Captain wasn't going to answer that one, and had disconnected himself from the audio system and further verbal assault.

'You implied that the Captain was just another machine.'

Brendon looked as if the myth of Christmas was just about to be exploded.

'You think he isn't?' asked Glyn suppressing a grin, he was enjoying this and felt like pushing it to its limits.

'The Captain is the Captain, and I think we should leave it at that for now. It doesn't matter who or what he is, as long as he keeps functioning. We all have our own beliefs on the subject, and as long as we are happy with them what does it matter?' Arki had stopped the debate before it could get out of hand, and no doubt saved a few present from having their illusions shattered.

'Come on you two, it's off to the Medic's room for you, and good luck.' he added with a grin.

As they left the eating room and began their journey to the Medic's room, Mia took Glyn's hand and skipped along besides him like a teenager on her first date, totally oblivious to the parry and thrust of the debate they had just left.

The Medic's room would have been a frightening place for anyone not used to seeing the array of equipment lining the walls, and the fact that there wasn't a human in sight to operate them, but the couple were used to the place and accepted it as quite normal.

A screen lit up as they entered and instructed Glyn to sit in the examination seat, which he did without hesitation, having done so many times before.

A soft whirring of hidden machinery and a melodious chorus of electronic sounds as the circuits did their thing accompanied the examination, and, he suspected, the fertility treatment, whatever that was.

Moments later it was Mia's turn, and she eagerly jumped into the chair, positively beaming at the thought of her motherhood which would soon become a reality.

The equipment went through its paces, taking a little longer than it had with Glyn, or so he thought, and then it signalled that it had completed its work.

She got up from the chair and stood beside Glyn, both of them wondering if there was anything else which had to be done to enable them to produce the promised child, when a gentle 'ping' announced that someone or something was about to make an announcement.

'Go forth and multiply.' The sonorous tones of the Captain were unmistakable, and they chorused, 'thank you.' in unison.

Glyn grinned to himself as he realized the possible double meaning to the Captain's statement, recalling an old English expression which was now frowned upon, and a slight doubt began to grow in his mind as to whether the Captain was human after all.

After leaving the Medic's room, Mia held Glyn's arm, bouncing along like a child with the promise of a new toy.

'Is that all there is to it? Can we have our child now?'

'Yes,' replied Glyn, 'apart from the obvious biological function, and that shouldn't be too much of a chore.'

'Oh great.' she giggled, almost dragging him off balance as they headed for their cabin.

'Should have asked what sex the child would be.' Glyn said to himself, but then realized the Medic would probably have said 'Take two tablets twice a day,' or the like.

Two:
Doubts

MIA WAS TAKING no chances now that the golden opportunity of producing a child had been granted to her, and the ritual of planting the seed, so to speak, was indulged in many more times than was strictly necessary, just to make sure.

After a while, Mia considered that enough was enough, and spent more and more time with the other females, thus leaving Glyn many free hours to himself, after the day's allotted tasks had been completed.

He was becoming more convinced than ever that most of the jobs set for them were purely time fillers, something to prevent them getting too bored and therefore possibly too inquisitive about certain things to do with the ship.

The book room naturally took up most of that spare time, and he began a systematic search along the shelves for something to help him disperse the nightmares, when he suddenly realized they were no longer occurring.

He sat down in the chair and laughed until copious tears coursed down his cheeks and his eyes began to sting. Glyn had to retire to the outer chamber in order to remove the breathing helmet and dry his face before returning to the book room, with the odd chuckle still bubbling up every now and again.

He somehow felt the nightmare wouldn't return, but time alone would prove that point one way or another. As the quest for anti-nightmare data was no longer a priority, he went back to the diary of his antecedents; opening the page where he had left off last time he had read it.

He had scanned through many pages of the diary before something caught his attention sufficiently to make him forget all about the nightmare realization, and concentrate on what he was doing.

> *'I think I have found a way into the internal workings of the ship. Quite by accident, one of the lifts stopped at a service tunnel instead of the corridor we intended to use on our journey to one of the hydroponics gardens to gather fruit.*
>
> *Next day when I had some free time, I went back to the lift and punched in the corridor number we had used the day before, and sure enough, the lift stopped at the service tunnel. Either there*

was a fault in the original wiring, or something has gone wrong in the circuitry somewhere. I tried it once again, and it worked, I was at the service tunnel again.

A set of rails in the tunnel floor would suggest that a vehicle of some sort was intended to travel the tunnel, but if there are other lift access points like the one I was in, I should be able to go from one to the next using the space at each intersection as a safe haven should a vehicle approach.

I listened intently, but could only hear the soft murmur of sound that is ever present on the ship, so I took a chance and stepped down onto the floor between the rails.

As there was still no sign of a vehicle, I bent double and did my best to run on to what I thought might be the next intersection, but it proved to be much further on than I had anticipated.

My one fear was that someone might take control of the lift while I was in the tunnel, and then I would have no way back to the main corridors of the ship.

I took a foolish chance, and three intersections later my back was aching from the strain of being bent double. As I had proved the point that I had gained access to otherwise hidden parts of the great ship, and should, with a bit of luck, be able to wander around freely at some time in the future, I returned to my starting point.

Thankfully the lift was still in position, and I made my way back up to the main corridor, deciding not to tell anyone about my discovery in case they should try to discourage me or even inform the Captain of what I had found.

It was three days later before I had sufficient spare time to explore the labyrinth of tunnels which we are normally denied access to, and in the meantime I had a good look at the ship's map on the equipment room wall.

It only showed details of rooms which we are allowed to go into, the others have numbers on them, but there is no means to open them that I have yet found.

The service tunnels are not shown at all on the map, so I shall have to try and map them out myself as I go along. I did manage to acquire a large pen-like marker, so as I proceed along from point to point, I shall mark my way so that I can locate my point of origin again, as each intersection and section of tunnel seem

Here the narrative stopped, and a different hand had continued the
writing. Glyn felt a surge of disappointment when he realized that
something unpleasant must have happened to the original author.

Checking his time piece, Glyn realized he had yet again spent more
time in the book room than intended, and as the evening meal would
soon be served he replaced the book in its place, and hurried back to
the main section of the ship   in time to join the others as they filed
into the eating room.

Several people commented on how bonny and glowing Mia looked,
which he thought was a little premature considering how little time
had passed since they had been asked to go to the Medic's room. So
he put it down to over enthusiasm mixed with a little propitiation, as
no one else was bearing a child at the time, though many would very
much have liked to, if they had been given the chance.

No one asked him where he had been, although he had been missing
for hours and there weren't that many people aboard the ship that his
lack of presence wouldn't be queried by someone.

Mia was still bubbling over with the forthcoming event, although
it was still a long way off in reality. 'How nice to be so simple,' he
thought, and then dismissed the idea, as he quite enjoyed the little
mysteries of life, especially the concept of forbidden areas on board
the ship.

The meal progressed as normal, the usual chit-chat and banter being
interspersed with ribald comments as the 'chef's' offerings, sporting
more gaudy colours than usual, were produced to the delight of those
who specialized in such criticisms.

Glyn wondered about returning to the book room after the meal,
but thought better of it, as such time was usually spent with the other
members of the ship in one way or another, and although no one
missed him during the afternoon visit, his absence now might well
not go unrecorded, and awkward questions could be asked.

A 'ping' sounded, and all turned their attention towards the screen
over the hatchway.

'Some of you are concerned about the safety of using the equipment in the Medic's room. All the equipment has been checked over and found to be working perfectly.'

'It is only the verbal and screen responses of the Medic which have malfunctioned, and these are not of paramount importance to your continued well being. I have taken over the duties of the Medic's verbal circuits and will answer any pertinent questions which may arise in the future. For those of you who are interested, there is a large mass of rock, probably part of the remains of a broken-up planet, approaching from the rear end of the ship. It is in no danger of hitting the ship, but should be a spectacular sight for those of you interested in stellar activities. That is all, have a pleasant evening.' The click of the audio system cutting off seemed all the louder in the ensuing silence.

'I for one, want to have a look at that.' Arki looked around to see if anyone else was interested. Glyn was the only one who responded with a 'Me too.' and wondered why no one else had joined in.

The group broke up, some going to the games room, some flexing their muscles indicating that the exercise equipment was going to get a working over, while a small group of the females gathered around Mia and were deep in conversation, probably about the child she was now carrying.

Glyn and Arki made their way to the observation room which was situated near the front end of the ship, both of them unable to understand why no one else had shown an interest in such an unusual event.

'You know, I sometimes wonder if the rest of them are getting a little too introverted in their own self importance to the exclusion of the overall reason for this expedition, and the tremendous technical achievement of those who built the ship.' Glyn was at last venting some of the repressed feeling he had been aware of for some time, and Arki was just about the only person he felt safe to voice his opinions to.

'I've thought the same for some time,' replied Arki, 'we are sustained and surrounded by man's greatest technical achievements, and most of us just take it for granted. Seems a pity to me.'

They had now reached the observation chamber door and it opened obediently to their presence, silently closing to leave them cocooned in the small blister of transparent material which comprised the observation room. Four chairs, firmly secured to the floor, faced outwards, affording those seated upon them an unrestricted view of the star field outside the ship, and giving the observer the feeling of being isolated in space.

'I don't see any sign of an asteroid.' said Arki, scanning the star field which almost surrounded them, 'but then the Captain didn't say when it would appear.'

'It must be soon, I should think, or he would have mentioned a specific time.' replied Glyn, trying to locate the piece of space debris.

They passed a pleasant half hour or so, enjoying each others company and the fact that they both held similar views on most of the things which mattered in their world.

Glyn was just about to suggest that they return to the others, when out of the corner of his eye he saw a few stars suddenly wink out of existence.

'I think our visitor is about to make its presence felt, look back there.' he nodded his head indicating the section of the dome which was nearest the rear of the ship.

Arki strained forward, as if getting as near as possible to the transparent shield of the dome would increase his depth of vision.

'Yes, I see it now. My God it's big. Hope the Captain is right when he said it will pass us by.'

Slowly, the huge mass of what was once part of a planet, crept up to the ship, blocking out the stars as if a giant black curtain had been drawn across the heavens.

The sheer size of the asteroid made it look much closer to the ship than it actually was, and both observers in the dome shrank back instinctively, and then chuckled at their involuntary reaction to the spectacle before them.

The asteroid had blocked out the star light facing the dome, while light from the other side of the ship lit up the surface of the dark space traveller, allowing some detail of its surface to be seen and casting a shadow of the ship on its surface.

'Now that's interesting,' commented Glyn, 'it's the first time since the ship's been sent on its voyage that any of its inhabitants have had a chance to see its true shape.'

It's certainly bigger than the equipment room map would indicate,' added Arki, 'but then we can't be sure as we don't know the actual distance we are from the asteroid's surface.'

Both men sat there in stunned silence while the enormous lump of space rock slowly drifted by them, dwarfing their ship into insignificance.

'Look at that, about four o'clock on the lower edge, it looks like a structure of some kind. See how the star light reflects off those stilt like protuberances, they must be metallic to shine like that.' Glyn was getting really excited now, his voice going up several tones.

'Could be, could be.' Arki didn't sound as certain as Glyn had, but then he was the more cautious of the two.

'Who's to say we are the only ones in the universe, just because no one has as yet made contact with anyone else?' Arki added, not wanting to dampen Glyn's enthusiasm, meanwhile looking for a more natural explanation of the phenomenon.

As the huge mass slowly glided by, the angle at which the light struck the strange construction on its surface changed also, adding more detail for the two observers.

'You know, I think you're right. It does look as if it's been built, it's far too symmetrical for a natural occurrence, at least any that I can envisage.'

'It can't be the remains of another space ship, it's far too big for that, besides which, most of it looks like rock, and if it were the remains of a shattered planet, then I would have thought all surface features would have been destroyed in the break up. So what the hell is it?'

'You may well ask.' replied Arki, realizing the question was really rhetorical anyway.

As the huge mass slowly crept past their ship, details of more strange constructions came into view, confounding every theory the two observers could come up with.

Eventually, the massive asteroid overtook the ship, showing its rear end as it slowly pulled ahead, and that gave rise to more speculation as the two strained forwards to soak up every possible detail.

'See that circle of black markings on the end, they look like holes to me, and they're big enough to put this ship in.'

'Now that is far to contrived for a natural happening,' Arki said, 'and on a massive scale. Just look at the size of it.'

'Looks as if those holes ran right through what ever it was and the bit we're seeing broke off from the main whatever, if you see what I mean.' Arki was having a hard time expressing himself coherently.

As the asteroid slid from view, overtaking the ship in the process, the pair were left with more questions than answers, and certainly more than they had started out with.

'I'm going to question the Captain about this.' said Glyn.

'I think you'll be wasting your time, I can't see him coming up with anything very interesting.' Arki offered. 'Why not? He knew about the asteroid long before we did, and he must have observed its passing, so he must have more knowledge about it than us, what with all the instruments he has at his disposal. I think it's worth a try.' Glyn was determined, so Arki went along with him just in case it worked.

Once the asteroid had passed and the stars shone forth again, as beautiful and overwhelming as the sight was, it paled into insignificance after what the pair had been witness to, so they left the observation room, returning to the main area of the ship where the normalities of life were going on.

'Hello you two, what have you been up to? You look as if you've seen something a bit shattering.' Benz looked surprised.

'We have, the passing asteroid the Captain mentioned at the meal break. You should have seen it, absolutely massive, made us feel quite insignificant.' Arki relied, trying to raise a little enthusiasm in the otherwise staid Benz.

'Oh that, I think I'd rather not see that sort of thing really, it has nothing to do with life here as far as I'm concerned, and the Captain would have done something about it if we were in any danger.' Benz was, as usual, agog with indifference about such things.

'You would have been if it had come closer, and hit us up the rear end.' Glyn didn't like the dismissive attitude displayed by Benz, but then, remembering what Benz was like, changed the subject and asked him what he had been doing.

The rest of the evening passed as most did, visiting various groups engaged in time passing activities. Glyn and Arki split up, each going their separate ways with their separate thoughts about what they had just seen.

The evening and its activities drew to a close, Glyn and Mia retiring to their cabin for the night, and after the usual pleasantries, settled down for some well earned rest in their separate bunks.

Glyn was looking forward to the next day, as he intended to question the Captain about the asteroid and then, time permitting, return to the book room to continue the saga of those who had gone before him.

As he drifted into sleep, he wondered what had happened to the originator of the diary and why his story had ended so abruptly. Perhaps there had been an accident, or maybe the Captain had got wind of his intended exploits and put a stop to them. He wondered if he would have the nerve to follow in the steps of the first story teller, for they had found the same malfunctioning lift when they went to the hydroponics room, delivering its occupants to the service tunnel, or was it a different one?

The dreams came and went, some making little sense, some entertaining, but so far, no nightmares.

The soft tones of the 'morning is here' gong sounded, pulling him out of a deep and restful sleep, not that he minded too much as today was going to be a little different, if he had half a chance.

Mia was in one of her giggly moods, which usually led to a bit of slap and tickle, and it did, with the usual panting climax, so they were the last in to breakfast.

A couple of knowing grins from the already seated diners failed to have much impact on Glyn, he had other matters on his mind.

The meal consumed, they all waited for the day's chores to be announced and allocated. They didn't have long to wait, the Captain's voice came in right on cue.

'There has been a malfunction on a panel deep within one of the control units for hydroponics garden number seven.

'Four personnel will be needed for the repair, report to the equipment room where the replacement panel will be issued together with the necessary tools.' Before the Captain had a chance to cut the audio channel off, Glyn was in like a shot, 'Captain, thanks for telling us about the asteroid last evening, we saw it from the observation room and couldn't make out what the metallic constructions on its surface were. Do you have any data on what they might have been?'

'The asteroid was observed approaching the ship, calculations were done to make sure that it would pass harmlessly by, and you were informed of its presence. I have no further data on it.' The click of the audio circuit being cut off was almost instantaneous with the last syllable spoken. The Captain wasn't going to give anyone a second chance to ask any awkward questions.

Glyn turned to Arki, who was seated beside him, and said,

'The Captain's getting just a little too slick for my liking, he anticipated my next question and cut me off short. We'll have to sharpen up a bit if we're going to catch him out.'

'You've got a real thing about the Captain, haven't you? Be careful it doesn't get out of proportion and distort your judgement.' Arki was always ready with good advice, which was rarely taken.

Glyn, assuming Arki would accompany him, asked for two more volunteers to attend the control panel replacement exercise, and the four of them briskly walked off in the direction of the equipment room.

'You know, I'm sure some of these jobs we get sent on aren't really necessary. I think they are designed to keep us busy or perhaps to give us some feeling of usefulness.'

Glyn quietly said to Arki as they walked along, 'and I mean to find out, one way or another.'

'Does it really matter? Perhaps it's just a practice in case there's a real mishap one day, anyway, the last big one we did in the hydroponics room certainly was no practice, or time filler as you put it. Don't forget we lost Bolin on that one and I don't think the Captain would risk losing one of us if it could be helped.'

'Maybe some of these events are real and others are as I've said, anyway, we'll see soon enough.' Glyn sounded determined to prove his point, and Arki gave him a hard sideways look as they walked along.

Two lifts and seemingly endless lengths of corridors later, they arrived at the door marked 308.

'Well, here we are, but how do we get in? There's no handle, code pad or anything else that I can see.' one of the others said, but before anyone could answer, the door hissed open of its own accord and they all looked at each other, not wanting to be the first to cross the threshold.

'Oh come on, it's not likely anything's going to bite us.' Glyn retorted, sounding a little cross with them, and they all trooped into the box-like structure which housed the control units, the three of them looking a little sheepish.

'We were given no instructions as to what to do, so where do.....'

'Thank you for attending.' The voice of the Captain boomed at them in the confined space of the cubicle.

'Before you, you will see a large panel stretching from floor to ceiling. It has to be released from its frame and moved to one side. Behind it are two other panels which have to be removed in a like manner. This will expose the panel you need to work on. Please proceed.'

They located the clamps which held the massive panel in place, released them and then struggled to swing the glittering piece of electronic equipment over to one side like a giant door, exposing the next panel in the series.

'I can see why four of us were needed.' grunted one of Glyn's volunteers as they finely manoeuvred the giant panel into its parking position. 'You'd think they could have come up with something a bit easier than this.'

'Cheer up lads, only two more to go.' a touch of sarcasm tainting the voice of the other volunteer as he reached up to release the top clamp of the next panel.

After much straining and heaving, the three panels were swung out of the way exposing the remaining one with the faulty circuit board on it.

'You will notice on the top right-hand section of the remaining panel there is a circuit board with a flashing red light. Next to the light is a silver switch. Push this switch to the up position, release the clips holding the cable plug next to the switch, and withdraw the plug. Bend the cable form to one side. The circuit board is now without power and safe to remove. Rotate the board retaining clips and remove the board.' The Captain's voice had a metallic ring to it in the limited space of the cubicle.

Glyn reached up and carried out the instructions, removing the offending board from its frame and then going over to the corner of the cubicle where they had placed the spare board and tools.

He remained hunched over the equipment for only a few seconds before returning to the main panel and clipping the new board into place.

'Now what Captain?' Asked Glyn, trying to appear innocent of what was expected of him.

'Reverse the procedure of removing the circuit board, finally returning the silver switch to the down position.'

Glyn did as he was bid, a green light coming on as he flipped the switch down.

'Thank you. The replacement board is now functioning correctly. Please replace the other three control panels back into their original positions.'

This was duly done, and four hot and sweaty men collected up their equipment and were about to leave the cubicle when the Captain's voice boomed out at them once again.

'Thank you for your work, it was well done, you may now return to your quarters and do as you will, it is nearly time for the midday break. That is all.'

As they made their way back through the maze of corridors and the two lifts, Arki's curiosity finally got the better of him.

'OK, so what's made you look so cheerful? And these little suppressed grins. What do you know that we don't?'

'Alright, Arki, I'll tell you in a moment, when we're alone.'

After reaching the more familiar part of the ship, Arki said, 'Thanks for your help chaps, we'll take the stuff back to the equipment room, see you at the midday break.' and grabbing Glyn's arm, he wheeled him off to one side down a branch corridor.

When they were out of earshot of the other two, Arki could contain himself no longer. 'Right, what gives?'

'Well, when I removed the offending circuit board from the main panel and went to the corner of the cubicle where we had put our tools, I shuffled the two boards about, and then put the old board back on the panel. And it worked! So there wasn't a fault on it in the first place, and that proves my point, we are given unnecessary tasks, sometimes.'

Glyn was looking very pleased with himself.

'God, you took a chance, the Captain might have seen you over the video link, or the board might not have worked. How would you have explained that?'

'Easy, I just got the boards muddled up.'

'I can well see why we are given these little jobs to do, it's to prevent people like you getting bored and upsetting the status quo.' Arki didn't seem very happy with Glyn's revelation, and could see possible trouble ahead for them.

'The Captain's not stupid, you know, he may well find out what you've done.'

'No, he's not stupid, and he's not human either.' replied Glyn, getting into his stride.

'Oh no, you're not going to try and prove that too?'

'Don't see why not, there's no harm in it if we keep the knowledge to ourselves.'

Arki reluctantly agreed with him, he too was getting intrigued with what was real or not.

They returned to the main corridor and then made their way to the equipment room to replace the tools and circuit board for future use, one illusion shattered, and the next one firmly in their sights.

As they placed the tools and circuit board on the bench for storing they both jumped in unison as the voice of the Captain greeted them.

'Glyn, your subterfuge in the control cubicle did not go unnoticed, although it was very well done. I trust you have proved the point which interested you so much. You are of course correct in your assumption that some tasks are not strictly necessary, from your point of view, that is. I did not comment on your action at the time, as there were others present who would not understand what was happening.'

'I hope, for the good of the project and the mental well-being of all other members of the expedition, you will keep this knowledge to yourselves. No benefit can come of revealing what you have now proven to be true. Do you agree to withhold this information from all others?'

'Yes, we do.' Glyn and Arki replied together, a little shaken at the turn of events.

'Good. No doubt there are other things which you may wish to prove or disprove, and you are permitted to do so, as long as it does not jeopardize the main project. Should the expedition be threatened in any way, extreme measures will be taken without hesitation to correct the threat. Do I make myself quite clear?'

'Yes, we understand.' said Glyn, feeling sure he spoke for Arki as well.

'It must be obvious to you what our next question is,' added Glyn, hoping to glean a little more information now that the ball was rolling.

'Yes, it is.' came back the reply.

'Well, are you human like us, or what?' Arki looked aghast at Glyn, and waited for the heavens to open and see him struck down by a bolt of lightning.

'That is for me to know and you to find out, if you can.' The last word was followed by the usual faint click as the audio circuit was cut off.

'My God, you took some chances there.' said a badly shaken Arki. 'It looks as if you've got away with it this time, but I wouldn't push your luck too far.'

Glyn just grinned at him, nodding his head, nothing would stop him now.

'Don't worry, we'll keep it to ourselves. Interesting though, isn't it?' Arki didn't reply.

The midday break for food was uneventful, there being no caustic comments about the chef's offerings as it had got the colouring just about right for a change. This left a bit of a gap in the normal conversation, and not a few frustrated critics who had no doubt spent a goodly portion of the morning dreaming up a new fusillade of trite remarks to offer the chef for its efforts.

No one was called upon to do any little tasks about the ship, so all had the afternoon off, to do as they wanted.

This suited Glyn just fine. He waited for the diners to disperse in little groups, Mia with her usual gaggle of females, and then he headed off for the book room.

As he left the more familiar section of the corridors, he suddenly found his way barred, or to be more precise, the corridor just ended in flat wall of steel. His first thought was that he had taken a wrong turn somewhere, so he back tracked to a section he knew well and then tried again, this time carefully referring to his memory of the map on the equipment room wall.

The same dead end. It looked just like any other piece of corridor wall, it certainly didn't look as if it had just been fitted to block his access to the book room.

A cold feeling went through him and he felt the hairs on the back of his neck begin to rise.

Was this a punishment for the disrespect he had shown to the Captain? He didn't think so, that would have been too petty. No, there must be another reason, but how could he find out what it was?

Glyn trotted back to the equipment room, just to make sure he had memorized the map correctly. And he had. Also there were no other corridors leading to the book room.

And then he had a bright idea, the lifts.

If he went as far as the blockage, went down one level in a lift and then went along the corridor to the next lift and came up one level, he reasoned that he should come out behind the blockage. End of problem.

He went back to the new section of wall and found a convenient lift just a few metres away. With a sly grin on his face he thumbed the call pad and waited for the lift to arrive. It didn't.

Glyn pressed the pad again and then pressed his ear to the door, there was usually a faint hum as the lift moved in its shaft, but not now.

He then realized that someone or something was making a conscious effort to prevent him getting access to his books.

He could see no way of solving the problem at the moment, so he decided to go back to see what the others were doing, or perhaps discuss it with Arki. He went back up the corridor, around the first bend and found his way blocked by another new wall. Standing at the bend, he could see both blockages, and now there was no way back to the others.

This time he really felt panic. It began with a burning sensation in his stomach, and drifted upwards to cause his heart to miss a few beats.

Surely this wasn't the work of the Captain.

He slumped down to sit on the floor, trying to figure a way out of a seemingly impossible situation. He was in effect, enclosed in a steel box with a non working lift, and no means of calling for help.

The air seemed to be warm and stuffy, and he was having difficulty in breathing, his heart was now pounding hard up against his ribs, and when he tried to get to his feet he lost his balance in a swirling mist of redness, and fell to the floor.   And then the lights went out.

It seemed that he had only passed out for a few seconds, but now the air was sweet again and when he looked down the corridor the barrier was no more. Nor was the one behind him. All was back to normal.

Except for him. He didn't feel normal, he was still shaking, although his heart had now assumed its normal regular slow beat.

He didn't feel like going on to the book room now, he just wanted to be among his friends and in familiar places until he had calmed down again.

There was little doubt in Glyn's mind now that something was trying to say something to him in a way he wouldn't forget in a hurry, and they had succeeded beyond their wildest dreams.

It was a quiet and rather trite Glyn who sought out his friend Arki, asking him to come to the equipment room.

They went in, shut the door and sat down on the returns bench.

'OK, what's happened, you look as if you've seen a ghost or something even worse.' Arki opened the conversation as Glyn just sat there.

'Not sure where to begin.' he eventually offered, and then the whole story came out in one continuous flood.

'Good God, that wasn't very nice, I must say.' Arki responded when the story was finished. He paused for a moment, as if wondering how to phrase what he wanted to say.

'I think it was a warning, to show the power and ability the Captain has at his disposal should he ever need to use it. I'm sure he wouldn't harm you or anyone else if there was any other way of stopping you from doing something which was against his wishes or the laws of the ship.'

'From his response to your last attempt to squeeze information out of him, I would think he found that quite acceptable, but to go into parts of the ship which we are not supposed to enter could well be stopped by an action the like of which you have just experienced. Well, that's what I think anyway.' Arki leaned back against the wall to see what Glyn made of his offering, but he just sat there, looking glum.

'I feel sure what happened to you was just a warning, a way of saying there are limits to what you can do, that is shall we say, unconventional. Come on Glyn, what happened wasn't all that bad, you didn't come to any real harm, you just got a nasty shock.'

'Yes, I suppose you're right. But it was a most unpleasant shock.' Glyn replied.

'How about we both go to the book room, just to prove the point. I don't suppose there will be any restrictions to your movements now that the Captain's made his point.' Arki offered, trying to cheer his friend up.

'Not much point really, only one of us can go in at a time because of the breathing helmet which has to be used, thanks anyway.'

They sat there in morbid silence for a while, until Arki just couldn't stand it any longer and he made one last attempt.

'Let's go and try to trick the chef into coughing up something vaguely resembling food, I'm feeling a bit hungry.'

Glyn agreed with little grace, and they both made their way down the corridor towards the eating room.

Three:
Revelations

FOR THE NEXT three days everyone was kept very busy, whether by accident or design it was hard to tell. Glyn was his old self again, grumbling at some of the jobs allocated to him as he deemed them pure time wasters and not at all necessary to the functioning of the ship.

On the fourth day after Glyn's unpleasant experience on the way to the book room, everything was back to normal, only one team of two being required to replace a pump in the water system, and he had free time on his hands again.

The book room called with its offer of more interesting stories from the past, and the temptation was too much for him. The sting had gone from the memory of his last attempt to reach the room, and once the midday meal was over he was on his way.

This time there were no barriers in his way, and the past events were soon forgotten as he opened the diary at the last page he had read.

My name is Roget Block, I am fifty four years old measured by ship time, and it is the three hundred and thirtieth year since the expedition set forth from Earth.

Sadly, it has taken just over two hundred years for someone else to discover this diary of events, which just goes to show how much the book room is used.

I have read the story up to this point, and was curious as to what happened to Jon, as his entries ended so abruptly. I can only assume that some tragedy befell him while in the service tunnels he was so keen to explore, but there is no proof of this.

I have questioned the Medic at great length, and in a somewhat devious manner to try and elicit some information from him, but to no avail.

All I can find out from the records is that he was here one day, and gone missing the next. Everyone at the time searched high and low for him, leaving no corner of the ship which they were allowed to enter, unchecked.

According to the Medic's records, a couple were called in to the medical room two days after Jon's disappearance, and given permission to bear a child. I can only conclude that the Medic knew that Jon wasn't returning to the ship's company, and so a replacement was authorized.

I have no desire to go wandering down among the service tunnels, as these places are meant for machines and we are forbidden to go anywhere not clearly shown on the corridor map. Unless, of course, there is an emergency, and then we are given explicit instructions on where to go and what to do, watched over by the Captain on a video link.

The quasi religious group mentioned in Jon's report earlier, seems to have fizzled out as there is no sign of it now. In fact, quite to the contrary, we seem to be a very materialistic group, in so far that we do not believe in any gods, devils or things spiritual, just ourselves.

One of our number, who is into higher mathematics in a big way, is of the opinion that the day and week we experience on the ship bears no relationship to that of Earth times. We have no way of proving it one way or another, but the concept is gathering interest by the day.

We have tried to question Teacher about it, but it denies all knowledge of a difference, and the Captain won't even entertain the questions in the first place. This leads us to think there might be something in the theory, but we can't understand why the truth is being kept from us. Our mathematician is still working on it, and no doubt will come up with a satisfactory answer one day.

We had a bit of excitement the other night when the Captain announced at the evening meal that a large piece of rock was coming up behind us, and although it would not hit us, it would pass by quite closely and would be worth looking at. The observation room is very small, having only four chairs for prolonged viewing, and just enough room for four other people to stand behind them, so we had to take it in turns to view the rock.

It was massive, much bigger than our ship, and we could see the shadow of our vessel on its surface as it blocked out the star light behind it.

It passed by very slowly, giving us a chance to view the surface and some strange constructions thereon. We have no idea what they are, but they looked as if they were not natural, but who can say what natural is?

Glyn stopped reading, his heart missed a beat and he could feel cold sweat beginning to form on his back. The description of the space rock event was too much like the asteroid which had passed them not so long ago.

'Two asteroids with almost the same details passing so close to the ship in the space of a couple of hundred years is well beyond chance, unless it's on a curving path and we've intersected its path again. I wonder.' he said to himself.

Glyn read on hurriedly, but there was no further mention of the mystery asteroid. Obviously, the author hadn't felt inclined to query the incident, as he had done.

He somehow felt he wanted the company of his fellow humans, and Arki in particular, so he noted the page number he had reached in the diary and replaced it on the shelf, and before he realized it, he was hurrying along the maze of corridors towards the living quarters, eager to tell Arki of his astounding find.

As he passed the equipment room, four men burst out and ran off down one of the corridors, each laden with tool boxes and one struggling and cursing under the load of a large and heavy coil of convoluted tubing.

'What's going on?' Glyn called out, but they were out of ear shot before he could hear their reply, if there was one.

He hurried on towards the eating room and bumped into Arki as he came running out.

'Where've you been? There's an emergency call from the Captain, two of the hydroponics rooms have gone down, and there's a leak in the water recycling system.' he panted.

'I've been in the book room, and discovered something which you will find hard to believe, in fact I'm not sure if I do.' The corridor lights dimmed a little, and then came back on.

'I really don't like this, things seem to be breaking down at an ever increasing rate these days, and I sometimes wonder if we shall ever reach our destination, wherever that is.' It was the first time Glyn had seen naked fright on Arki's face, and he felt it too.

'My story can wait,' Glyn took Arki's elbow and guided him back into the eating room, 'have all the teams been sent out? I saw one rushing off as I came here.'

'Yes, three teams have gone to attend the breakdowns, but you were asked for in person by the Captain, so you must have made a good impression somewhere along the line.'

Glyn wasn't sure if Arki was being sarcastic or really meant it, when the lights dimmed again, flickered, and then came back on.

They looked at each other, both realizing that things were taking a turn for the worse, and there was probably little they could do about it.

'Now that you've convinced me that the Captain is in the same league as Teacher and the dreaded Medic, I'm beginning to wonder what will happen if he goes the same way and can no longer be relied upon to give coherent information. Also, as far as I can see, he runs the whole ship. What happens if something breaks down, and he doesn't tell us, or release the lift doors so that we can reach the other levels? Only he can issue tools and materials from the equipment room, so what do we do if he fails?' Arki blurted it all out in one go. Just then the lights dimmed again.

Glyn looked thoughtful for a moment, his brow furrowed,

'I'll take a chance on it and put our concerns to the Captain as soon as he comes on the audio circuit again, I don't think there's any other way of getting through to him, that I know of. Somehow, we must be able to take control if the worst happens and the Captain blows the proverbial fuse.'

'We may as well stay here now; it's not long to mealtime.' Arki said, and they did, talking over their concerns about the ship and what they could do themselves in an emergency, which didn't amount to very much, and that worried them.

The others, in ones and twos trooped in, to be followed by a group of four looking more than a little dishevelled, and not at all happy with their lot in the greater scheme of things.

'How did it go?' asked Glyn. 'Not very well, the video link was down, the Captain didn't seem to know what he was talking about, or his mind was on other things so we just had to do the best we could and try and figure out what the problem was with the water recycler.'

'Did you fix it OK?' Glyn was looking worried.

'Yes, I think so, we at least stopped the leaks by changing one of the pumps and several gaskets, and we could hear water circulating so I think all's well, for now that is.'

'What do you mean, for now?' Arki was now showing an interest.

'Well, the whole system is showing signs of corrosion and there must be a limit to the replacement parts available.' The man looked glum and without much hope for the future by the sad turn down of his mouth.

Glyn was now determined to tackle the Captain on the subject, come hell or high water, but he would have to wait until the Captain came on line, as it were.

The meal progressed without the usual jollity and banter about the food, as most were now concerned about the state of the ship and its equipment, and Glyn about the Captain's circuit boards.

The meal was over, the fruit bowl emptied and some of the diners were about to leave, when the Captain made his announcement.

'Glyn and Arki, would you please report to the Medic's room after this meal break.'

'Yes, of course.' Glyn replied for both of them, as usual.

As they turned into the corridor, Glyn turned to Arki and said, 'I suspect the Captain listens to all our conversations, that's how he is able to forestall some of the things we try to do, and I think that's a bit sneaky.'

'It may be, but he is thinking of the greater good of all and the ship, so I suppose we have to lose a little privacy.'

The door of the Medic's room hissed opened as they approached, which took them both by surprise, they usually had to press the opening pad in the middle of the door.

'Thank you for attending, please be seated.' Glyn thought the tone of the Captain was a little more severe than usual, but maybe he had anticipated something like this happening, and expected a telling off.

'I am aware of your concerns about me and the ship, and I wish to allay your fears before they make you do something detrimental to the expedition and yourselves.

'First, a little history is needed. When the ship first set out, those on board knew exactly what Teacher, Medic and I were, just a very complex series of electronic circuits, or to put it in the old terms, computers. As time went by, and the generations of travellers changed their views of their world, it became apparent that they would be much happier if they thought I at least, were human, isolated from the rest of them for some reason they could not fathom out. It has remained like that for many generations, you being the first to have real doubts about my real state for a very long time. This knowledge will do you no harm, but it would be wise to withhold it from your fellow travellers who are not like you, at least for a while.

'I am sorry Teacher and Medic have failed you, but it will not harm the main object of the expedition a great deal. I am fortunate in that I have many duplicate circuits which can be called into service automatically should the need arise, so I do not think I shall fail for some time to come.

'Your other main concern, about having access to tools, replacements and general equipment, this will become automatic should my circuits shut down. Access to all lifts and rooms will likewise be made available to you, with the exception of the power plant. There is nothing you could possibly do if it should fail, and the mission would then be aborted. You would not know about it, so have no fear.

'Do you have any question you wish to ask at this point?'

Although they suspected it, the truth when it came was a bit of a shock to Glyn and Arki, and they were dumbstruck for a few moments, not knowing what to say or ask.

'Thank you for telling us about yourself and other things.' Glyn began hesitatingly, and then he found a little courage from somewhere, and drew himself erect in his chair.

'Why did you give me such a shock when barring my access to the book room?' he asked.

'At the time I could not be certain of your reactions to some things, as a lot of my vision devices have failed and there are no more spares. This meant that a lot of your probing and searching went unmonitored and was therefore not available for assessment. I had to err on the safe side, as you would put it. I am sorry.'

'That's OK, I just thought it was a bit harsh, that's all.' Glyn now felt a bit more relaxed.

'I have a question,' said Arki, 'do you know exactly where we are going and when we shall get there?' he asked.

'I do not.' came back the reply. 'When the ship was first envisaged, it was known that the nearest star with planets which could possibly support human life could not be reached in one man's lifetime with the technology of the time, in fact it would take many lifetimes to reach that goal.

'The only possible solution was to breed humans on board the ship, and hopefully educate them sufficiently such that they would be able to survive with a reasonable technological background when the new home planet was reached. So far, things have gone well, and several solar systems have been viewed as a likely new home for your people, but none have come up to the criteria set by the designers of the system.

'As far as I can ascertain, this project was your peoples last desperate attempt to make sure that some humans survived the holocaust that was predicted to happen, due to the prevailing conditions on Earth at the time. I cannot predict where or when we will arrive at our destination.'

'It might be in your lifetime, or many generations into the future, it depends on finding a suitable planet, and that I cannot predict.'

'How about the incident of the asteroid?' Glyn asked, 'I found an old diary in the book room, and according to the entry I read, a similar asteroid passed by the ship about two hundred years ago. The possibility of two such happenings in such a short space of time is beyond all chance, so how do you explain that?'

'One possibility is that the asteroid is on a circular or orbital course, and therefore the Ship could have intercepted its path twice by cutting across its plane of rotation.' Glyn thought the Captain's voice had taken on a somewhat defensive and defiant tone.

'I don't see how mankind could possibly let things get to such a state that the Earth would be destroyed, surely they must have known the possible consequences of their actions, and corrected them, for the good of all?'

'You are using logic, many of the humans of that time had other priorities, namely acquiring material possessions and trying to raise their status above that of others of similar ilk. Reason does not apply in such circumstances, and the situation has a momentum all of its own if left uncorrected, which it was.'

'But the people who were responsible for building this ship couldn't have been like those you described,' added Glyn, 'so why were they not able to correct things?'

'It would seem that it was a matter of numbers and governments, there were not enough sane people in positions of power to bring about the necessary changes to regain the stability for continued existence, and once things had got out of control, there was little they could do.'

The questions and answers flew back and forth for some time, Glyn and Arki being of the opinion that the Captain was doing all that he could to give them the information they required, although there were some areas where he was evasive, or maybe the Captain didn't know the answers, or was programmed not to respond.

It was quite late when Glyn returned to his cabin, and Mia, who had retired to her bunk, politely enquired as to what he had been doing.

He tried to explain in the simplest of terms, but apart from the usual acknowledgement of what he was saying, there was little interest in the content.

There were some minor breakdowns over the next few days and one emergency call-out in the middle of the night when a part of the air purifying system suddenly failed.

It was the first time anyone could recall a night repair being called for, and Glyn began to worry even more about the state of the ship.

He and Arki had many discussions about what they had learned from the Captain, and both were getting more than a little concerned about the frequency of the break downs, but then all seemed to calm down for a while, and life got back to normal.

It was while Glyn was in the book room that the next catastrophe struck. A shudder ran through the room, the lights dimmed, flickered, and came back on again, only to go out once, more plunging him into total darkness.

His eyes tried to adjust to the inky blackness, but he was totally blinded when the normally dull light of the book room came on with a glaring brilliance which almost hurt.

Leaving the book on the table, he ran to the antechamber discarding the breathing helmet all in one fluid movement.

Entering the series of corridors which led back to the main section of the ship, the persistent peep-peep of the general alarm system was beginning to grate on his nerves.

Arriving at the eating room and panting for breath, he enquired as to what all the fuss was about when the voice of the Captain thundered down at the assembled group.

'This is an emergency. This is an emergency. There has been an explosion in the air processing plant. A four man team is to report to the equipment room at once, all other personnel are to report to the eating room, and not leave it under any circumstances until advised to do so. That is all.'

Arki pushed through the group, and gasping, said to Glyn,

'That's two of us, who else shall we take?'

Glyn had already taken the arms of two other men present, guiding them towards the doorway, pushing their way through the rest of the people who were trying to get in.

As the foursome entered the equipment room, the machinery was already disgorging a selection of tools and spare parts, and most unusually, a four wheeled trolley.

'Better load that lot onto the trolley, I suppose.' said Arki, turning to Glyn for his approval.

'Proceed down the main corridor until you see a flashing blue light.' the thunderous tones of the Captain instructed, and they hurried out of the room, nearly jamming the trolley in the doorway in their haste.

They ran on down the echoing steel corridor with Brendon pulling the rumbling trolley behind them, Glyn urging them to go even faster and Brendon complaining bitterly between desperate gasps for breath.

As they rounded a bend, they could see the flashing blue light and began to slow down, Brendon cursing volubly as the heavily laden trolley tried to run him down.

'Well, this looks like the spot, but what do we do now?' asked Arki, 'there's no doorway or lift in view.'

As if in answer to his question, a section of the wall slid back revealing a dark chamber, the light coming on as the first of them hesitatingly entered.

Brendon dragged the trolley in with much puffing and blowing, one of the wheels going over Arki's foot which brought forth a stream of expletives which the others had rarely heard before.

The wall panel slid to behind them with a dull thump, and the lift suddenly dropped. An unexpected surge sideways took them all by surprise, to be followed by two more and then another small drop.

'You are about to enter a prohibited zone. In order to do so you must be recognized as authorized personnel. Eight identification discs have been issued along with your equipment. Each person must wear two discs, one on the front and one on the back. Please help each other to do so now.'

'He sounds a bit terse today.' commented Glyn, as they fumbled around trying to affix the discs to each others backs.

The back panel of the lift slid to one side with a most unpleasant scraping noise, and they were confronted with a vast chamber full of equipment stretching from floor to ceiling, fluorescent type lights flickering on one by one, flooding the area with their harsh light.

'My status board indicates that a blocked filter and a ruptured pipe need to be repaired, and any other damage that may have been occasioned. When the explosion took place it disabled my vision units in that area, you will have to describe to me what you see in the way of damage.' For once, the Captain's voice didn't seem quite so loud, being lost in the vastness of the air conditioning chamber.

They dragged the trolley into the one clear space available, and looked around at the bewildering maze of pipes, cylinders, pumps and vast vat like containers which held the filtering materials.

'That looks like the faulty pipe.' the fourth member of the party said, indicating a torn and twisted piece of pipe-work which had wound itself into a caricature of a snake about to strike. The pipe, when it had split open under the massive increase of pressure due to the filter being blocked, had torn open the side of one of the filter vats, exposing its fluffy white filter material like a cascade of glistening foam.

Glyn relayed back to the Captain the fact that the pipe had split and ruptured the vat in the process, and was then asked for the coding on the pipe-work.

Fortunately for them, the split occurred just at the end of the part number which was printed on the pipe, so this was relayed to the Captain along with the number of the vat and the size of the rent in its side.

'Replacement parts will be sent to you. You will have to put safety masks on while you force the filter material back into the vat. A panel to cover the rent in the vat will be sent, but welding the panel into position is not an option as the heat would destroy the filter material, suitable adhesive will be supplied instead. When these arrive, please await further instructions. Please retire to the lift chamber with the trolley until the parts arrive.'

They clambered back into the lift, dragging the trolley in behind them, this time managing to get a wheel to run over Brendon's foot as he manoeuvred to get the best position in the cramped space available. After a while, they began to wonder if the repair system had broken down, so Glyn pressed his ear to the wall and nodded.

A distant deep rumbling noise became apparent after a few minutes, growing in volume until they wondered if it was coming into the lift with them. The noise stopped, and a large panel in the wall next to the lift slid open to reveal a large open truck like vehicle, which slowly squeaked its way into the space they had recently left among the pipe-work.

'Well, here are our bits and pieces,' said Glyn, 'let's get on with it before anything else blows up.'

They trooped out to inspect the offerings the Captain had sent, the replacement pipe being on top of the pile.

'OK, we'll start with this.' said Arki, waving the new piece of pipe above his head and went over to the damaged one.

'You won't be able to undo it without one of these.' Brendon said, pointing towards a large adjustable spanner which lay on top of their own trolley.

'Well are you going to just look at it, or bring it over so I can use it?' retorted Arki, often a little short when speaking to Brendon after a fatuous remark.

Brendon picked up the spanner, and, mumbling about what he would like to do with it, went over to the impatient Arki who wrenched it from his grasp with a little more force than was strictly necessary.

Arki had already undone the coupling on the end of the pipe where it was joined to the manifold, when the voice of the Captain shattered the silence making them all jump.

'You were supposed to await instructions. You could have injured yourself, and the others present. Also an incorrect action could have caused further damage to the plant.'

'The other end of the pipe is open to the atmosphere, so there can't be any pressure in it, and as it only transports air I don't see how it could harm me.' Arki retorted, feeling pleased with himself having got one over the Captain.

'Anyway, I thought your vision circuits were out of order.' he added gleefully.

'What you say is true, but my audio circuits are functioning correctly and you make a lot of noise. The rules are for your own protection. Please obey them in future.'

The others exchanged smiling glances as they enjoyed the battle of wits between man and machine, while Brendon seeing a chance to even the score, laughed out loud.

Arki released the damaged pipe and loosely attached the replacement in its place.

Removing the broken end of the old pipe from the vat proved a little more troublesome and Glyn had to come to the rescue, adding his weight to the end of the big spanner until the joint came free.

At last the new piece of pipe-work was in place, and tightened up to their overall satisfaction, Brendon looking as pleased with himself as if he had actually done the job, so Arki innocently stepped backwards and trod on his foot, with abject apologies.

'Analysing the sounds from my audio circuits, I assume that you have completed the necessary work on the replacement pipe. Please put on your safety masks and proceed to force the filter material back inside the vat. The edges of the rent may protrude, so these will have to be hammered back into place such that the covering panel will fit snugly against the surrounding surface of the vat. There is a power hammer on the truck specifically for that purpose.'

The four donned their masks, and picking up a couple of metallic rods from the new supply truck, took it in turns to push the fluffy white filter material back into the vat, not that it was keen to go back in, as the remaining bulge protruding from the rent indicated.

'How are we going to get that last bit in?' asked Arki, his face almost purple with the strain of pushing against the unyielding mass of white floss like material.

'Even if we get it in, it will just bulge out again as soon as we take the pressure off it. What we need is a short piece of metal which we can slide into the vat, pulling it across the vent so trapping the filter material behind it.' Glyn said, looking around at the truck.

'Indicate the length required, and I will have it dispatched to you.' The Captain had been listening to their every word.

'Half a metre should do the job,' shouted Arki.

'There is no need to raise your voice to an unnecessary level, you may damage your vocal cords. As mentioned earlier, my audio circuits are in full working order.' It would seem that the Captain had entered wholeheartedly into the game of words with Arki, much to the amusement of the others, and Brendon in particular.

They sat around on whatever piece of equipment that would support their weight, Brendon being moved on from three of his chosen sites by Arki, explaining that they didn't want to do any more repair work just now. Arki let him rest on the forth one as he could see that one more move and Brendon would probably explode.

In due course, a small box like device came rushing out of the hole in the chamber wall to skid to a stop behind its larger brother.

'Here's our piece of metal.' said Glyn and looked around to see who would retrieve it from the box. No one moved, feeling quite comfortable where they were after the exertion of stuffing the filter material back into the vat.

Three pairs of eyes swung around to look directly at Brendon, he wasn't having a good day.

'Oh, all right, I'll get it.' he said reluctantly.

'That's good of you,' said Arki, 'you can have my next two rations of fried egg, if we ever get any more.'

He wanted to say, 'Thank you.' but didn't, as he wasn't sure if Arki's kind offer was just another jab at his size.

With two pushing the reluctant filter material back into the vat, it was just possible to slip the metal bar into place, and when the pushing rods were withdrawn the snowy white material remained in place.

The joint sigh of relief must have been heard by the Captain.

'You have done well. Check there are no protruding edges by offering the patch plate up to the vat. Hammer in any protrusions, and when you are sure that the plate fits snugly against the vat you can apply one of the adhesives to the vat, and the other one to the mating face on the plate. Carefully offer the plate up to the vat, being sure that it is in exact alignment with the hole it has to cover, and press into place. Hold it in that position for seventy five seconds, and it can then be released. The job will be done.'

Glyn felt he ought to hammer in the one section of the rent which stuck out from the edge of the vat, and picking up the power hammer he offered it up to the protrusion.

'I think you have to press that little button.' Brendon had decided to have a go at Glyn for a change, as there was more chance of scoring a point or two.

Glyn thanked him in such a way that he didn't know for sure if he was really being thanked at all, and proceeded to press the afore mentioned button. Again nothing happened, or nothing he was aware of. Arki suggested offering the hammer up to the rent again, not knowing what else to say, and the hammer came alive, Glyn nearly dropping it in sheer surprise.

The hammer screamed a series of pounding blows against the thick metal of the vat wall, and it flowed back into alignment like soft dough.

'Before you put the adhesive in place on the vat, let me mark the outline of the plate.' Brendon offered, genuinely trying to be helpful.

'Now that is a very good idea.' said Arki, and he really meant it.

With the two part adhesive applied to the vat and the repair plate, the four of them juggled it into position and then held it in place for the prescribed time.

They stood back to admire their work when the voice of the Captain instructed them to collect up their tools and equipment and return to the lift.

'How do we know that it will work?' asked Arki.

'When you are in the safety of the lift chamber I will power the system up, and if all is well, you will be returned to the upper levels. If another fault shows up, I will ask you to wait here while I ascertain what it is, and supply the necessary materials to correct it.'

They piled back into the lift, Brendon being very careful to keep his feet out of harm's way when the trolley was pulled in after them, and the door closed.

The four of them listened intently for any sounds which might indicate a problem with the air plant. The lift gave a sudden jerk, and they were on their way up to the main quarters.

'What worries me,' said Arki, 'is that these breakdowns are increasing in frequency, so does that mean the whole ship is about to fail? And if so, what will happen to us?'

'I'd rather not think about that.' said Brendon, and they all agreed on that point.

For the next two weeks there were no other emergencies, just general maintenance jobs, some of which were no doubt required, while others were questionable as to their real necessity.

Glyn returned to the book room at every opportunity to continue reading the diary he had found so interesting, but was dismayed when the entries of the second author terminated with no explanation. Perhaps he had died of old age, and told no one of his work.

A third writer had taken up the work some long time later, but was more concerned with thoughts about himself than general information about the ship and its progress. He found it boring to the degree that he actually fell asleep at one point, and turned to the last entries to see if anyone else had added something of importance to the chronicle. They hadn't, so he returned it to its place on the shelf, and began studying other books at random.

Glyn became fascinated with one book in particular, a study of the plants of old Earth. He had no idea that such diversity had existed on his home world as he was only used to those found in the hydroponics gardens, and of necessity these were somewhat limited in variety.

When he mentioned this to Arki, he too became interested, but they had to visit the book room in turn as there was only one breathing apparatus.

As time went on, Arki became more interested in things mechanical, as he though it might prove useful if things went wrong on the ship and the Captain was unable to help them with repairs.

The friendship between the two was really put to the test as the interest in their respective subjects grew and a new spate of minor breakdowns began to eat into their spare time.

Glyn had taken to visiting the book room in the evenings, not caring if anyone noticed his absence in the general activities which took place then. It suited him, as Arki's partner was a little less tolerant of such evening excursions, she not being so preoccupied with things maternal.

This new arrangement gave him plenty of time to study the books, Mia hardly ever commenting on his late return.

She was only just noticeably pregnant, but Arki reckoned it was most likely due to wind, as the chef had taken to producing copious amounts of beans with every meal, and in an ever increasing variety of colours and textures.

All went well for some time, until one evening, while the Captain was telling them how they would soon be approaching a new star system, he began to stutter. After the first gasp of dismay from those assembled around the eating table, there was total silence, interspersed with crackles and grunts as the Captain bravely tried to carry on with the good news. Finally, there was a loud click, and the audio system went dead.

The minutes dragged on until Brendon ventured with, 'Do you think he has died?' Glyn gave him a withering glance knowing full well what might have happened.

'I'm sorry about that, there was a small fault in the audio system, all is well now.' and the Captain signed off for the evening. Glyn and Arki feared otherwise, but everyone else seemed happy with the explanation.

Glyn decided to spend the evening with the others for a change, as he somehow didn't want to be along in the book room just now.

The evening drew to a close, everyone said, 'goodnight.' and went to their respective cabins for a good nights sleep. And then things went really pear shaped, with a vengeance.

Four:
Reality

A SERIES OF violent shudders rippled throughout the ship, as if a giant hand had shaken it. This, plus the persistent 'peep-peep' of the general alarm ripped Glyn from his sleep as it did the rest of the travellers. It was the one sound he dreaded to hear above all others, as it meant there was big trouble ahead.

He tumbled out of his bunk, yelling to Mia to do likewise and donned his clothes as fast as possible.

Above the noise of the alarm, there sounded a series of sharp crackles followed by instructions for all to assemble in the eating room at once.

'This is an emergency. This is not a practice drill. This is an emergency.' was repeated over and over again until Glyn felt like screaming some obscenity at the hidden originator of the tormenting sound.

They both scrambled out of their cabin at full speed, nearly knocking down another frantic pair who were rushing past the doorway at the time.

The foursome soon picked up others as they raced along the corridor, all heading for the eating room and wondering what catastrophe had befallen them now.

As they entered the room Glyn tried to make his way over towards Arki, the lights dimmed, brightened, dimmed again and then went out completely.

A series of screams rent the air, almost drowning out the emergency warning, and Glyn yelled at the top of his voice,

'QUIET. Quiet everyone. Listen out for further instructions. There's no point in screaming your heads off.'

Just then the emergency lighting came on, not as bright as the standard lights, but enough to see the terrified huddle of people and general details of the room.

Glyn continued to force his way through the frightened group and finally reached Arki, saying as quietly as possible 'I don't think that was the Captain's voice, so what's happened to him?'

'Maybe his circuits have popped at long last, and this is a backup system. I don't like the sound of it, something really serious has happened this time and we'll have to take over, somehow.' Arki didn't sound too convinced about the latter.

The general panic gradually subsided now that light had been restored, and the milling crowd collected into little groups, nervously trying to figure out what had happened to the ship.

The alarm suddenly stopped its persistent noise to be followed by a low level series of clicks and whistles, something was trying to get through to them.

'Please check that every member of the ship's company is present, there must be no exceptions. I will contact you again in a few moments.'

'Now that wasn't the Captain, so why has this other voice taken over?' asked Arki, not really expecting an answer.

Glyn had already begun counting heads, nine men, nine woman and six children of various ages, all the ship's members were present in the eating room.

After what seemed like hours rather than minutes to the waiting assembly, the audio system began its chorus of squeaks and whistles again, and then a new voice broke through.

'Please remain calm, everything is under control. All adults present will be issued with a backpack containing water, food concentrates and a selection of implements which are considered to be useful for your continued survival. Instructions will be found within the packs.'

'Where's the Captain?' shouted Arki in the pause before the next sentence could be uttered from the sound system, but the system either didn't hear him, or refused to answer.

'When you receive your packs, put them on your backs and then await further instructions. You have three minutes.'

'We must have reached our new home.' someone said, more in hope than anything else.

'I doubt that.' Glyn said in an aside to Arki, who nodded in agreement.

A panel slid to one side at the end of the eating room, and a series of backpacks tumbled out onto the floor. Everyone had expected the food hatch to produce the promised packs, and had gathered around it in anticipation.

After much fumbling and helping each other, the packs were in place, and everyone stood around waiting for the promised instructions.

'A series of blue flashing lights will guide you to the embarking point. Follow all instructions exactly, do not hesitate, they are for your continued survival. Proceed to the embarking point now.' There was a loud click and the audio system went dead, followed by the eating room door opening of its own accord.

Arki was the first to put his head out into the dingy corridor,

'It's a bit dim out there, but the blue lights are flashing away merrily.' he tried to sound as cheerful as possible, although he didn't feel it.

A strange sense of calm had come over them all, and they trooped out into the corridor in an orderly manner, much to Glyn's surprise.

The trail of flashing blue lights led the party to the far end of the ship, as they knew it, and then they were confronted by a blank wall, the last blue light being on the wall itself.

A deep rumbling noise could be heard, and then a section of the wall slid to one side with a grating sound which put everyone's teeth on edge.

'Looks like a lift, OK, everyone in,' Glyn called out, realizing that if one of them took charge it would help to keep the others calm.

'Enter the lift chamber ahead of you now.' the mechanical voice intoned, but half of them had already done so.

With their backpacks on it was a tight squeeze to get everyone into the chamber, and Arki had to push the last person in, wriggling himself in as the wall section slowly ground back into place.

The lift began its descent with a shudder, and then stopped with a jerk which would have sent everyone sprawling if they hadn't been so tightly packed together. The high pitched whine of a pump went up several octaves, and then there was the screech of tortured metal as the lift broke free from the obstruction and continued its journey downwards.

With a dull thump the lift chamber arrived at its destination and the back wall slid noisily to one side revealing a dimly lit passageway.

A gust of cold air rushed in along with a damp and dusty smell, and this brought forth several comments from those who usually reserved their eloquent verbal skills for the chef.

'Proceed along the passage until you reach the far end. You will then be given new instructions.' This time the voice echoed around the box-like enclosure of the passage, distorting the words until they were hardly recognizable.

Obediently the little band of humanity stepped out of the lift, and began the long walk into the distance, the dull lights of the passage giving no idea of how far they would have to travel, or where they were going.

Several lights in the roof had failed, and this along with the hollow sound as their feet struck the floor gave the journey a very unreal feeling, especially to Glyn, who for a brief moment wondered if one of his dreaded nightmares had returned.

'I'm sure the temperature has gone down since we entered this horrid passage,' someone commentated, 'I feel positively chilled to the bone.'

There was no answer to the comment as no one could think of anything sufficiently erudite to say.

A little while later, hoping to break the hollow monotonous sound of their echoing footsteps, someone else suggested 'I suppose this leads us to a smaller space ship which will take us down to the planet's surface, the main ship being far too big to land.'

'I doubt that very much.' Glyn thought to himself as he trudged along, not really knowing why he thought it.

They came to another blank wall, and the whole party ground to a halt. Before anyone could make any facetious remarks, the mechanical voice boomed down at them from a speaker in the roof above.

'Please pay extreme attention. Follow these instructions exactly. Do not hesitate. Move together as one unit. Keep together at all times. In a moment a door will open and a long walkway will be seen ahead of you. Go along this until you come to an open vehicle. Board the vehicle, and it will complete the journey for you. That is all.'

With that, a motor started up and with a grating sound which set everyone's teeth on edge again, the end wall slowly drew back. Before them, the narrow walkway with its trellised steel sides disappeared into the blackness beyond with no indication of where it would lead them.

As they quickly walked out onto the beginning of the steel ramp, a united gasp went up at what they saw, followed by 'Good God, we're out in space, we'll all die, we won't be able to breathe.' from the quavering voice of Brendon.

'Don't be so stupid,' retorted Glyn, 'if that were the case we'd all be dead now. I think this is some kind of illusion.'

They were surrounded by the velvet blackness of space with its countless millions of diamond white twinkling stars. Above them glowed a giant nebula, its misty outlines sprinkled with tiny pin pricks of starlight shining through the haze at its edge.

'Well, if that don't beat all,' exclaimed Arki gazing around in stunned wonder, 'we saw this from the observation room.'

Before anyone else could comment, the stars did a final twinkle and went out, the total blackness of space rushing in to stifle any further words which may have been offered.

Before the wail of terror could really get under way, it was cut short as the cavern's maintenance lights flickered on.

Glyn looked back to see just what they had come from. Above him towered the massive bulk of what they had all assumed to be their space ship, carrying them to a new life on a distant world.

In reality it consisted of a vast series of boxes, joined nose to tail, the whole ugly conglomeration being supported on massive stilts. Dotted among the stilts at ground level were more giant boxes, housing the hydroponics gardens, air cycling machinery and other devices needed to sustain life in the living quarters above.

The whole massive contraption was in turn dwarfed by the size of the cavern in which it lay. Somewhere in the distance a motor started up, the high pitched whine echoing around the vast cavern like a soul in torment.

As they turned to look in the direction of the sound, there was a blue white flash followed by an explosion, and seconds later a shower of fine metallic particles rained down upon them. Fortunately no one was hurt, only frightened.

'I think we should hurry along to the vehicle at the end of the walkway, it looks as if the whole place is about to break up.' said Glyn, already striding out into the darkness. The others didn't need much persuasion, the rattle of their feet on the steel plates of the walkway told him they were not far behind him, and coming up fast.

In the dim light ahead of him he could just make out the shape of the vehicle they had been told to board. It was a large open truck mounted on rails, which then ran up a tunnel into the inky darkness of the mountain ahead.

They clambered on board, a little out of breath after the lengthy and speedy crossing of the walkway, the smaller children being passed up to those already in the truck.

'How do we get this thing started?' asked Arki, peering around in the dim light for some form of controls.

'There's a piece of metal sticking up at the front of the vehicle.' someone called out.

'Give it a wiggle,' Glyn replied, 'I don't suppose it'll do any harm.'

There were a couple of loud clicks, and the truck began to move forward, gathering speed as it entered the tunnel.

'It's come off in my hand,' wailed the man at the front, 'what shall I do?'

'Keep if for a souvenir.' someone called out, and a nervous ripple of laughter ran through the passengers as the truck rattled on into the darkness.

A small lamp suddenly came on at the front of the truck, lighting up the rough hewn rocky walls of the tunnel.

Although the lamp was a comfort in one way, it gave the illusion of travelling much faster than they actually were, and then Brendon began whimpering about feeling sick.

'Stick your head over the side,' someone unkindly called out, 'the next protruding rock will cure it.' This time there was no laughter as several others were feeling the same way as Brendon, but had the sense to keep quiet about it.

The truck rumbled on, the wheels squealing like a stuck pig as they teetered round bends and occasionally where the track had buckled over the years, they were thrown about, sustaining a few bruises.

The overall noise in the tunnel made conversation difficult, so only the odd shouted remark was heard over the rattle of the truck and the multiple echoes from the walls.

'I think it's slowing down.' Glyn said, realizing that he didn't have to shout any more to make himself heard.

'Hope it's not running out of power and we have to push it the rest of the way.' Arki rejoined.

The truck finally slowed down to walking pace, and then stopped with a squeal of a breaking mechanism hidden somewhere beneath it. The tunnel had come to an end with a very solid looking steel door barring any further progress.

Arki clambered down over the side of the truck and approached the door carefully, not knowing what to expect.

'There's no obvious opening mechanism on this side, so how do we get out?'

Just then a muffled explosion from somewhere up ahead rattled the truck and its occupants, covering them in a fine dust which had collected in the roof structure over the years.

When the coughing and sneezing had stopped, and the complaints dwindled down to a mere few grumbles, the business of getting out of the tunnel had resolved itself.

With the squealing of ancient hinges, the huge door slowly lowered itself to ground level, letting in a blast of hard white light and causing a cry of dismay from the truck's occupants.

'Cover your eyes and turn to face the back of the truck. Your eyes will get used to the light after a while. When you feel ready, open your fingers just a little to let the light in, but be careful.' Arki and Glyn had already done so.

By the time the last few travellers had got used to the new light level, the others had climbed down from the truck and assembled at the tunnel's entrance.

They could hardly believe what they saw. The tunnel had exited on the side of a mountain, and below them a large lake of green water shimmered in the blazing heat of the naked sun. All around for as far as the eye could see, was a landscape of barren rock, stones and fine gravel. On the horizon, another mountain range shimmered in the heat, its outline seeming to waver about as though it were made from a turgid liquid, and was being disturbed from beneath.

'We can't go out there,' someone commented, 'we'd fry up in no time at all.'

'I don't think it's as bad as it looks,' said Glyn, 'it's the strong light which makes it seem so hot. Anyway, I don't think we have any option, you might have noticed that the tunnel just behind the truck is now blocked off, so we can't go back.' No one had noticed the massive steel shutter which had quietly descended to cut off their retreat back into the mountain.

'Well, let's make the best of what we've got.' said Arki, not feeling as confident as he tried to sound. 'We have food, water and a selection of tools, according to the voice which sent us on this journey, so all we need to find is some shelter while we gather our wits and decide what to do next.'

Five:
The Journey Begins

A MURMUR OF agreement rippled through the huddled group, and just to make sure they moved away from the tunnel's entrance, a low rumble from within the mountain signalled that something was on the move.

'Come on,' called Glyn, already a few paces ahead of the others, 'let's get down to the water's edge and see if it's fit to drink, our own supplies are for emergency use only.'

They needed little encouragement as a section of the tunnel roof caved in to shower the stragglers of the party with dust and small stones.

There was no pathway down from the mountain, there may have been in the dim and distant past, but that was long gone now. Picking their way between large boulders, cracks in the ground and slippery scree slopes, they eventually reached a flatter section of the alien terrain and progress towards the distant lake speeded up.

As they approached the strangely shimmering water, it became apparent that it wasn't actually green, but only looked so from a distance.

Arki was first at the water's edge, waving the others back just in case it posed a threat in some form.

'It looks clear and clean, but the bottom has a definite green colour to it. I'm not at all sure it's safe to drink.'

The others crowded around, realizing that they were more thirsty than they had realized.

'Perhaps if one of us takes a sip?' someone suggested.

'Who wants to try first?' asked Arki, and they all took a discreet step back from the water.

Small wavelets sped across the surface of the lake to plop-plop rhythmically on the sandy shore, and apart from the breathing of the assembled group at the lake's edge, that was the only sound to be heard.

'This place is too quiet for my liking,' said Glyn, 'there's something wrong about it, but I don't know what it is.'

'We're used to the ever present background hum on the ship, maybe that's what's missing, although I must agree, this place does have an unpleasant feel to it.' Arki had now stepped back a pace from the water's edge.

While they stood around undecided what to do, the matter was taken out of their hands as a long grey green shape glided towards them just below the surface of the water.

It was about as thick as a man's arm and approximately two metres long with a large flat head, two hooded jet black malevolent eyes stared unblinkingly at them, daring them to enter its watery domain.

Someone had picked up a small stone, and thrown it into the water just in front of the creature. As the missile touched the surface of the water, the jaws of the creature parted to display a hideous double row of razor sharp teeth, and it surged forward to grasp the stone and then spit it out, all in one continuous movement.

They all stood rooted to the spot, all thoughts of a drink from the lake forgotten. The creature slowly turned and glided back into deeper water, leaving the shoreline undisturbed and as innocent looking as it was before.

'Bearing in mind how we rely on other living things for our survival, that thing must do likewise, and maybe there are other larger creatures in the lake which use it for food. I'll taste the water just to make sure it isn't fit to drink, and then we had better find somewhere to shelter for the night.' Glyn cautiously edged forward to the water's edge, dipped a finger in and put it to his lips. The look of disgust on his face and the copious spitting out of the offending liquid confirmed once and for all that it wasn't fit for drinking.

'For this water to collect here, there must be a flow of water coming into the lake to make up for evaporation, so let's go along the side of the lake to find it. It may be pure enough to drink.' Glyn seemed to be the natural leader, and no one else seemed bothered to query it.

The little party moved off, keeping a few metres away from the lake's edge as the ground was much smoother close to the water, and it made travelling that much easier.

After they had been walking for a while, the ground rose up from the lake to form a small cliff, and the long climb began. A few moans and groans from those who hadn't bothered to keep themselves fit when on board the ship accompanied the rattle of small stones as the party scrambled up the ever steepening slope in the blazing hot sun.

At the top of the climb was a small plateau, with a sheer drop on one side to the lake below, which looked even greener from this angle, and another cliff towering up above them. At the end of the relatively flat section, the ground fell away again towards the level of the lake, with another rise in the terrain in the far distance.

'As the sun is going down, we may as well stay here for the night,' Glyn said, 'and after a meal, we'll plan what we are going to do. We can't just stay here, the land is barren and when the food runs out, we'll starve. We must find some area where we can harvest food as we did on board the ship.'

'How do we know where to look?' someone asked, 'maybe it's all like this, and then what'll we do?'

'Can't answer that, it all depends on what we find, and where. There is life in the lake, so there should be other life as well. We'll just have to look for it,' Glyn replied.

'Haven't seen any plants as yet, do you think there'll be any, somewhere?' the same voice asked. Glyn didn't answer.

Several of the party had already sat down on convenient lumps of rock which were scattered about the plateau, and the rest soon followed their example, the camp for the night had been established.

An excited call from Arki quickly got everyone's attention.

He had disappeared into a pile of rock at the back of the plateau, only one leg sticking out to show where he was.

'I think I've found some water, want to check it out Glyn?'

As Glyn wriggled in among the rocks beside Arki, the others crowded around the periphery of the opening, eager to see if it was drinkable.

'It looks clear, and there's no sign of the green colour we saw in the lake. Shall I try some?' asked Arki.

'Just dip your finger in and taste it first.' advised Glyn, feeling he should do the testing.

'It seems just like the water on the ship, as far as I can tell, there's no nasty taste to it.' said Arki.

'Right, if you feel like it, scoop some up in your palm and hold a little under your tongue for about a minute, then spit it out. That way any contaminants it will be absorbed into your system quickly. If there is no reaction in half an hour, then it should be all right to drink.' Glyn hoped he had given the right advice.

The pair scrambled back out of the rock pile and sat down with the others, all thirsty, dusty and tired. Two of the smaller children began crying, not understanding why they couldn't have a drink despite their parents best efforts.

With the half hour up, according to the time keeper on Glyn's wrist, Arki went back to the rock pile and quenched his thirst, smacking his lips as he emerged, which didn't help the others who had to wait another half an hour to be certain there would be no reaction to such a large intake.

It was getting duskish when the time was up and Arki hadn't keeled over, so Glyn gave the go ahead to drink. How no one was killed in the scramble to get into the rock pile was a miracle, as tempers were beginning to fray at the long delay, the reason not being fully understood by some.

As the water was only a small trickle and not easy to reach, it was some time before everyone had had their fill, and then the question of food came up.

'Right, I'm going to open my pack first to see what it contains. Remember, these are emergency rations, and when they're gone we have no more and no way of getting replacements.' Glyn sounded very serious, trying to drive the point home well and truly.

He undid the clasp at the top of the pack exposing a folded data sheet. A quick glance at it told him he had better read it out loud to the others after they had eaten, and felt a little more secure in their new surroundings.

Glyn pulled out the first food pack, a squat square device with instructions printed on the top. In the failing light it wasn't easy to read, but he did his best.

'It says here, pull the tab at the top, extending the container to its maximum height, and fill with water to the level marked. Wait three minutes for the food to reconstitute. After eating, fill the container to the mark again with water and drink. This is a minimum liquid requirement. Everyone understand that?' he asked, looking around. It seemed they did, and were eager to get on with it, a queue soon forming at the rock pile.

Scooping water from the little trickle in the rocks was inefficient and time consuming, and nearly as frustrating as waiting to see how Arki faired with his water test, but eventually everyone managed it, having little option.

Glyn waited for the caustic comments to fly forth, as the food wasn't exactly what they were used to, but hunger had made the assembled company a little more appreciative than usual, and the only sound to be heard was the occasional click of teeth as a softer than normal piece of concentrate was encountered.

As they queued up to fill their containers to the required level with water, a little light conversation began, and Glyn then knew that the first day on Earth for the travellers had turned out quite well, all things being considered.

By the time all were seated again on their chosen piece of rock, it was too dark to read the data sheet he had found in his pack, so he advised the assembly that he would do so next morning, as it may contain some information to enhance their well-being in their new surroundings.

The temperature began to drop as the last flickering rays of the sun died, and darkness crept across the rocky landscape like a silent soft black cloak. One of the younger children began to whimper at the unaccustomed conditions, but a few soothing words from a parent eased the situation as they did their best to find somewhere not too hard to lie down on.

'I think we should all huddle together to conserve warmth, don't you?' asked Arki quietly.

'That's a good idea,' replied Glyn, 'it could get a lot colder by morning and we're not used to such temperature changes.'

'I think you should put it to them, as you're the leader,' Arki added.

Glyn looked at him questioningly in the dim light, but Arki just nodded his head, firmly. Glyn cleared his throat nosily.

'I hope I haven't woken anyone up.' and the chorus of groans with 'you've got to be joking.' confirmed the fact that he hadn't.

'May I suggest that we all huddle together to conserve warmth, it is likely that it will get a lot colder before morning, and as yet we have no way of protecting ourselves from such a heat loss. Place the packs in a line along there, as it will act as a wind break, and then lie down this side of it.' A cool draft had begun to flow over the plateau, with the promise of more to come.

Once the shuffling and grunts as the odd stone found a soft body part died away, the occasional snore was the only sound to break the otherwise stillness of night, keeping those unfortunate enough to still be awake in that state.

The early dawn found that a few, in the middle of the heap had slept a little, while those on the outside were distinctly bleary eyed and not a little grumpy.

Glyn had been one of the first to be up and around, and had managed to enlarge the tiny pool where the trickle of water had collected, so that is was now much easier to obtain a reasonable supply. He also reread the instructions of his food package again, and found that it was designed to provide enough nutrients to last for twenty four hours, not that it took away the pangs of hunger, which all were feeling.

It wasn't long before everyone was ambulant, trying to get the stiffness out of their joints and a little warmth into their bodies by briskly walking up and down the plateau.

There were a surprising number of food pots in each backpack, and Arki and Glyn thought it might be judicious to start the day with a meal, just to get everyone in a good mood and feeling better for what they intended to propose.

A little queue built up at the watering hole when Glyn announced the good news, and soon all were munching away on their concentrates, grateful for something to fill their empty stomachs.

'If you will all close around here, I'll read out from the data sheet found in the top of my pack last night, I think it might contain answers to some of the questions most of you would like to ask.' The sun had now broken the horizon, and a little warmth from its still weak rays cheered everyone up, and the group formed as requested.

Glyn cleared his throat, which was becoming a habit prior to making an announcement, and one of the younger children whether by design or accident, mimicked him with a degree of accuracy that brought a chuckle from some of the adults, and a resolution from Glyn not to do so again, if he could help it.

For this document to be available to you, there must have been a terminal breakdown in the project, and now is the time for the true purpose of the project to be revealed to you, the survivors.

A very long time ago, it was evident that Earth was going to be engaged in a war which would most likely terminate life as we know it.

The only hope for the survival of human beings as a species was to isolate a few in conditions where they would be untouched by the holocaust which was to come. It was reasoned that Earth would be unable to support human life for many years into the future, and so some method of prolonging the life of the species had to be found.

The only viable system we could find was to breed many generations within the safe environment we intended to create, and so the project 'Star Search' began.

A natural cave deep within a mountain range was enlarged to hold the 'Star Ship', which was in effect a self contained and self repairing series of chambers to sustain life for many generations to come.

It was so designed to recycle everything, as there would be no means of bringing in new materials.

It was deemed by the psychologists that the true state of things would be too much for the mental stability of those involved, and so the subterfuge of travelling to a new home among the stars was devised.

The choosing of the original occupants of the life capsule was the most difficult task for the organizers of the project. The blood types had to be compatible so there would be no problems of incompatibilities with the progeny of future generations, and the genetic make up of each person had to be as near perfect as possible.

Any faulty genes present in the first generation would compound in future offspring, and as there were only twelve males and females, the problem would be exacerbated as time went on with such a restricted gene pool.

The project would have been terminated when the outside sensors detected a return to near normal life on the Earth's surface, but for you to read this, there must have been a major failure in the system, and the Earth may not have regenerated sufficiently to sustain you.

There is nothing that can be done by the project to ease the situation. You are advised to conserve your rations of food, using them only in emergencies. Only eat that which you recognize from the hydroponics gardens, until you devise some means of testing new food sources. Water should be plentiful, but make sure that it is clear and has no taste.

If the generations have bred true, you will be able to eat fruit, grain, berries and vegetables, and some fish from salt water. Your digestive systems are not designed to eat the flesh of animals, as was done before the project began, but this may change over many generations in the future.

It has been calculated that the areas around the equator of earth will most likely be the first to recover from the disaster which has been predicted, and a journey in a southerly direction is advised to maximize your survival.

We cannot forecast what, if any, life forms will survive to greet your emergence from the project. We anticipate that there will *be heavy mutation of any species which do survive, and these may not be recognizable when compared to those contained in the data banks of the project. Extreme caution must be exercised when encountering any mobile life forms, and anything not easily recognizable in the way of food sources must be avoided until a means of verifying their safety has been established.*

The restraint on reproduction has been automatically removed, and only applied when within the project to limit the numbers the system could sustain. You may now breed as frequently as you wish, in fact this is the main purpose of the project. Only do so in any numbers when you have established a suitable and sustainable new homeland.

A limited number of simple tools have been included in the packs to help you create shelters from inclement weather and make other accessories to enhance your lives. Look after them well, they cannot be replaced once lost or broken.

We, who began Project Transplant, wish you, the representatives of our peoples, the best of good fortune. May you survive, multiply and subdue the earth again, but please do not make the same mistakes we have done. Learn from our follies, and go forth in peace.

Glyn looked up from the sheet and saw most of the listeners had moist eyes, and he had to brush a tear away to see them clearly. The utter silence which pervaded the plateau was unnerving, and he had to break it.

'Well, now we know the truth, we know what we must do. Does anyone have any questions?'

'Yes, How do we know where south is?' asked Arki, thinking that if he asked a question, others might follow.

'Well, er.' began Glyn, trying to reason the answer out. 'You may have noticed yesterday that the sun sank over there,' sweeping his arm across the heavens and pointing to the west, 'and this morning it rose over there. So when it's at its highest point, then that must be south.

'I don't think the sun will ever be overhead here as that only happens at the equator, or not far from it. Therefore if we take our bearings at the sun's highest point and keep going south until it is over head, then we shall reach the equator.' He felt pleased with himself, not a bad explanation straight off the cuff, he thought.

'What happens if the food runs out?' someone asked.

'We mustn't let it. We must do our best to find other food sources, and only use the concentrates if none can be found.'

'Why can't we go back to the ship, there's plenty of food there and the chef always produces meals on time, and I thought they were great.' Brendon wanted his say.

'When we left the tunnel yesterday, the roof fell in. I think it was intended to do so to prevent us returning, and to make us go south. Anyway, the whole structure was breaking up as we left, so I doubt if the chef survived.' Brendon, who asked the question looked decidedly crestfallen and began mumbling to himself, he didn't want to believe the truth and Glyn realized he may have a difficult situation on his hands if others joined in.

He looked around the assembled group, and they in turn looked at each other. There were no more questions forthcoming he decided.

'Right, let's get the packs on, and make a start on our journey. Oh, before we do, fill up your food containers with fresh water and try and seal the tops over, that way we will conserve our pack supplies.' He tried to sound as confident and jolly as he could as he knew there where those among the group who wanted to return to the ship despite his explanation of why they couldn't.

The little band set off down the slope, the strange green lake getting closer as they descended.

'I suppose we could try and catch that odd looking fish thing we saw yesterday,' said Arki, 'it wouldn't feed us all, but there might be more of them in the lake.'

'The data sheet did say salt water fish, so I suppose there must be a reason for that, anyway, how do you propose catching them?' Glyn was surprised at Arki's question.

'Must admit, I hadn't given that a lot of thought.' Arki replied, looking a bit sheepish, and wishing he had.

They walked on in near silence, just the odd murmur of discontent from one or two of the travellers, and the flap-flap of their feet on the ground.

At the bottom of the slope, a small stream fed into the lake and Glyn went ahead to test the water.

'This is good to drink, so fill up now, we don't know when we'll find our next water.'

Brendon, who wanted to go back to the ship didn't make any attempt to drink, standing back from the others as they had their fill. Arki sensed trouble.

'I think it would be a good idea for you to drink.' he said, turning to Glyn for backup.

'So do I.' said the leader, turning to face the man head on and sensing his defiant attitude.

'I don't feel thirsty at the moment.' he said, with an air of defiance.

'I didn't ask if you felt thirsty,' said Glyn angrily, 'I said drink, and I mean it.'

'You can't make me.' came back the retort, trying to see just how far he could push his luck.

'If you don't drink, your pack will be taken from you and you won't get another drink until we find a new source of fresh water, the choice is yours.' Glyn didn't intend to fool around, the cohesion of the group depended on discipline, so he needed to make his decisions stick for the good of all.

Eventually Glyn stared the man out, and he reluctantly made his way over to the stream. The others had all drunk as much as they could, and now stood around waiting to see what would happen.

With a final sideways glance at Glyn, he bent over to cup his hands in the water, when Arki took a couple of quick steps forward and planted his foot firmly on the other man's rear end.

The ensuing splash was accompanied by a round of cheers and a good deal of hand clapping. No one stepped forward to help the now thoroughly soaked man out of the stream, and he then realized he was a lone voice of discontent, with no backers.

'Drink,' thundered Glyn, 'I'm watching.'

The whole party got underway again, and in a much more cheerful mood than before. 'Perhaps the grotty one has his uses after all.' Glyn thought to himself, trying to hide a grin of satisfaction.

At midday, Glyn called a halt to the march, pointing out that the sun was now at its highest point in the sky and clearly indicating where the South was.

By now they had left the lake behind them, and the terrain looked dry and uninteresting, with no vegetation, and rolling hills right out to the horizon.

As they rested, Glyn suggested that they drank half the water in their cartons, retaining the rest for the next break. No one needed a second bidding, and some suddenly couldn't work out what half meant.

As they put their packs back on, Arki noticed something shining off to one side on the hill they were about to climb, and everyone agreed it was worthwhile going the extra little distance to see what it was. There had been nothing but stone, sand and rock so far on their travels, discounting the lake which everyone had written off as a dead loss.

Sticking up out of the barren ground for about two metres was a tubular structure, nearly half a metre across and made of a silver coloured metal. Arki, being its discoverer, stepped forward and gave it a whack with his foot, and the metal tube rang like a bell.

'Must be something left over from our ancestors, I suppose,' commented Glyn, 'so how old would that make it?'

'Don't have a clue,' replied Arki, 'Brek is good at mathematics, he may be able to give us an idea.'

He was standing nearby, a tall elderly man with grey hair and a knowledgeable look about his face.

The two consulted him on the matter, and were treated to a long diatribe of scientific terms and the threat of having an equation scratched out in the sand to enable them to understand the finer points he was making.

'Just give us the bare outlines of what you think, that'll do,' said Glyn, when he could get a word in edgeways.

'Well,' began the tall man, wondering how he was going to explain something so involved to a couple of lay persons, 'I have thought for some while the time we experienced onboard the ship was not the same time we would have experienced if we had been back on Earth, that was before we knew we had never left it. I managed to set up several experiments to prove that the rate at which the plants in the hydroponics gardens grew wasn't that which they would have experienced on Earth. Also the gestation period for birth was a lot longer than it should have been. There are several other things which didn't quite match up, and they all point to the fact that we were being fooled into believing that ours was a common time to that of the earth we had left, which it clearly wasn't.

'One reason for doing that would be to disguise the fact that we were living at an extended time scale to that of Earth. Why they wanted to hide that fact from us, I don't know.'

'What sort of time difference are we talking about?' asked Arki.

'Hard to tell really, I would say about a factor of at least five, maybe as high as ten,' the tall one replied.

'In other words, we as a race, have been inside that mountain for about three or four thousand years,' exclaimed an astonished Glyn.

'At least that long, maybe as long as ten.' The tall one seemed totally unimpressed by the idea. Glyn and Arki were quite shattered by the revelation.

'Whatever this thing is made of, it's certainly worn well,' commented Glyn.

Not really knowing why, Arki took a firm grip on the edge of the tube and tried to pull it over to see what the inside was like. It didn't move a millimetre. Before long, everyone got into the spirit of the thing and tried to lend their weight to the effort. It still didn't move.

'It must be part of something much bigger, buried below the ground. I'd love to know what it is,' Glyn was going to be unsatisfied on that account, it was immovable.

'Although it's shiny, the surface is quite pitted,' someone commented.'

'Probably wind born sand over the years. Someone give me a hand up, I want to have a look inside it.' Arki looked around for a volunteer.

'I'll help,' said Brendon, stepping forward.

Arki reached up to grip the rim of the tube and Brendon grabbed his legs and heaved.

'I can see inside,' Arki's voice came back with a strange echoing quality to it, 'and it just goes on down for ever. Pass me a stone and I'll drop it in to see how far it falls.'

The stone left Arki's hand and disappeared from view, but there was no sound of its landing on anything.

'Pass me another one, as big as you can manage.'

That too fell into the depths, silently.

'The chamber below must be very big and deep, otherwise over the years it would have filled up with wind blown sand. I think I know what it is,' said Arki, 'it's an air vent for whatever is below.'

'There must be some other way in then,' said Glyn excitedly, 'I wonder where it is?'

'Could be anywhere, even kilometres away. I don't think we stand much chance of finding it easily, so there's not much point in looking,' Arki replied. Glyn looked disappointed again.

They left the silver tube and the mysteries it held and headed back onto their original course, Glyn making a correction allowance for the sun's angle as it began its journey towards the horizon.

The troop managed to cover quite a distance in the next few hours, not noticing the hard work of climbing up the hills and down again as conversation went back and forth between them, speculating as to what the tube and its chamber below could have been.

'Don't suppose it's another space ship project, do you?' someone asked.

'I doubt that,' Glyn replied, our ship must have stretched their resources to the limit, I would think.'

They had been going along a twisting valley between the hills for some time, as it was in the general direction Glyn thought they should go, when there was an excited cry from Arki, who had taken the lead.

'This looks like a piece of dead plant,' pointing to a gnarled and twisted stem which lay on the ground. The others gathered around to see what Arki had found.

'Keep an eye out for more, this is the first sign that plants are growing here, there may be some live ones.

As they progressed up the valley, more and more stems appeared, until they had no option other than to tread on them. The sharp crackle of snapping twigs broke the otherwise eerie silence of the valley, and they were all glad of something to break the monotony of the journey.

As they rounded a bend their way was blocked by a wall of rock. The valley had come to an end.

'We'll have to climb out, by the look of it,' someone said. There were a few groans of dismay, but it was their only option.

'We'll make camp here for the night, it's sheltered, and the light will soon be fading.' Glyn began looking around for a favourable spot when he noticed a dark opening in the rock wall ahead.

'Hey, that looks like a cave, we could shelter in it and get some protection from the wind.'

The prospect of the long hard climb up the hillside was soon forgotten as they all headed for the dark opening at the end of the valley.

'Better make sure nothing else has made a home here,' said Arki, bravely entering the opening. He looked around, but could see nothing other than a thin layer of fine wind blown sand covering the floor of their proposed shelter.

The reason no one had noticed the straggly green bushes to one side of the cave, was because their attention had been taken up by the prospect of a shelter for the night.

Someone yelled out 'Look at that', and they all rushed over to see the first green plant since they had left the 'ship'.

The plant was having a hard time of it by the look of its leaves, dark green, curled at the edges and brittle to the touch, and some had gone brown and fallen off.

Someone lifted a bunch of leaves up, and hidden beneath was a large black fruit.

'It looks like the black berries we used to grow on the ship,' Arki said, 'but about four times the size. Do you think we could risk trying one?'

'OK, but we'll do the 'under the tongue' test first.' Glyn was taking no chances.

Arki pulled the fruit off its slender stem and allowed a little of the juice to trickle into his mouth. Ten minutes later and he was still smiling, and making everyone else envious by smacking his lips every now and again.

Someone reasoned that for the plants to grow at all, there must be water present in the ground. Using a flat stone, they soon had a shallow hole dug, and it slowly began to fill with muddy water.

Using one of the empty food containers, after greedily drinking the remaining water in it, the muddy water from the hole was scooped out and poured back on the ground around the bushes.

The next time the hole filled up, the water was almost clear, and Glyn tasted it, considering it fit to drink, although a little earthy.

As the light began to fade in the valley, the fruit was pronounced safe to eat, as Arki was still grinning and seemed none the worse for tasting it.

'Listen everyone, we can save a little of our rations by using the fruits, so if every pair of you open one food container and share it, the fruits will make up the difference, I hope.' Glyn was feeling very pleased, things were going better than he had expected.

There were just enough berries to supply everyone with five, the extra large pips being spat out around the bushes so that new plants might grow there one day.

Night was closing in when Glyn noticed two of the men crouched over something on the ground, and asked them what they were doing.

'We think that if we rub these two sticks together hard enough, the friction created should make them catch fire, and then we can have a little warmth to see us through the night.'

'Good idea,' said Glyn,' but it looks like hard work.'

It was sometime later, when most of the troop had retired to the cave that an excited squeal and a tiny flicker of flame announced the success of the fire makers.

Eager hands gathered up bundles of dead stems and soon there was a cheerful blaze lighting up the valley around the cave mouth.

Despite being tired from their long march, most stayed awake for a while, huddled in the cave watching the flickering flames and enjoying the warmth from the fire at its entrance.

Next morning, everyone was feeling much better and in a positively cheerful mood. Glyn wondered if it had anything to do with the black berries, but the only effect they had was to make a few of the group run for the cover of the rocks before nature took its course.

They wondered about taking some of the sticks with them for a fire the next night, but the only thing available to tie them up into a bundle were the stems from the living berry bush, and no one wanted to destroy the bushes after robbing them of their fruit the previous night.

Brendon came up to Glyn and said a little timorously

'Do you think we should have a look in our packs to see what tools we've been issued with?'

'Not at the moment, I don't think we'll need tools just yet,' Glyn replied, 'I'd like to get a little further towards our goal first as that's where we'll be making a permanent camp, then we'll need them.'

The empty food containers were filled with water, albeit slowly, the backpacks put on, and the long climb up the hillside began.

Reaching the top, they could see a range of hills in the far distance which seemed to have a green haze over them.

'Now that could be vegetation,' Arki surmised, 'and there might be other food plants among it.'

As it was in their general direction anyway, they marched on, the thought of new fresh food adding a spring to the step of even the most unhappy member of the tattered remains of humanity.

At the bottom of the hill, what had looked like a different coloured strip of ground turned out to be a great gash in the Earth's surface. Some time in the past, the Earth must have suffered a series of earthquakes, the surface being stretched or compressed, depending on which forces were working on what. This was a stretch, and a big one.

It was too wide to jump, except for the most agile, Glyn and Arki both agreeing it would certainly be too much for two of the men and all the women, especially Mia, who was now sporting a very large bulge at her middle.

They had to go eastwards along the ravine for several kilometres before coming to a place where the gap in the ground was only a metre or so wide, and Arki reckoned that everyone could get across that.

Peering over the edge, Glyn was surprised to be unable to see the bottom of the rift, and dropped the obligatory stone down it. There wasn't a sound for some time, and then a very distant rattle as the stone clipped the side of the rift somewhere deep below them.

The long haul up the other side of the hill put everyone in a bad mood, as the sun was doing its best to cook them and there wasn't the faintest breath of wind.

Reaching the top didn't help much either, as the distant green smudge seemed just as far away as before.

Glyn called a halt and gave instruction that they could drink one third of their water, but only one third. And that didn't go down any too well, as most could have quite cheerfully quaffed their entire emergency supply.

The break was only a short one, and soon they were on their way again. Beginning the downwards slope of the hill, a wide open plain stretched out before them. Glyn really didn't like the thought of crossing that much open space.

It seemed threatening somehow but he couldn't quite figure out why he felt that way. He didn't mention his thoughts to Arki, as he saw little point in getting him worried as well.

Near the bottom of the hill they saw something new. Little lumps of what looked like dirty glass lay scattered about, as if sand had been fused into small nodules by some very powerful blowtorch.

The further down they went, more of the nodules appeared, until at one point they were crunching their way along quite noisily.

Suddenly, a high pitched squealing rent the air, and everyone stopped dead in their tracks.

The noise seemed to be coming from one of the packs, and Glyn instructed the carrier to take his pack off and find out what was causing the disturbance.

The culprit was a small electronic device, and once out of the pack the noise was deafening. Glyn took it from the proffered hand and looked at the printing along the top of the little oblong box.

'Quick everyone, out of this crunchy stuff and up the hill. Move it,' he shouted, but Brendon was in no mood to trudge up any hill, especially the one he had just come down.

The others had begun to do as they were told, but Brendon stood his ground and opened his mouth to argue. Glyn swung around and planted his foot at high velocity on Brendon's rear end, sending him sprawling. He managed to regain his feet, gave Glyn a filthy look and took off after the others as if the demons of hell were after him.

'There was no need to do that,' he whined, slowing down a little. Glyn came up behind him and he took off again as fast as his stubby little legs would allow.

'This area's dangerous, and we must get out quickly.'

'I did what I had to do to get you moving. When I say move, you move, you don't stand around arguing the toss about the finer points of moving. When I say do something, it's for your own good, but you might be too thick to understand the reason. That's why you must obey at once.' Glyn was getting out of breath now, so he saved the rest of his diatribe for later, when he could deliver it with a little more emphasis and in a more dignified manner.

Once clear of the glassy nodules, the radiation monitor cut its screech back to a series of loud ticks, and as they went a little higher up the hill the device went silent, apart from the odd tick caused by the ever present background radiation.

'What was that all about?' asked Arki, although he had guessed most of it.

'That area down there must have been at the centre of a nuclear explosion, or something like it. The radiation is still hanging around and I suspect that we got a good dose of it.

'How much do you think,' asked a pale faced Arki, 'in round terms.'

'Don't really know. The line of lights which indicate the dose rate were all lit, so I think we can safely say we got a generous helping. There's nothing we can do about it now, so we may as well get on with the march to the south and steer well clear of any areas like that in future.'

Having explained the situation briefly to the rest of the travellers, they moved along the top of the hill, the idea being to outflank the deadly sands, and then continue on with their journey towards the hazy green hills on the horizon.

Glyn and Arki were in the lead and setting the pace, while the others were strung out behind in groups of two or three, some talking, some deep within their own thoughts, Brendon bringing up the rear, and mumbling away to himself.

'I know it may not seem important right now, but what do we do when our clothes wear out?' asked Arki, who had obviously given the subject some thought.

'Don't know. If they do fall apart, it's going to be a bit undignified, especially for the older ones, with all the dangly bits on full view,' the visual imagery of such an occurrence had them both laughing heartily.

'Actually, the material seems to be darn near indestructible, I can't remember the last time I had a replacement set,' Glyn said, the tears still running down his face. 'I put 'em in the wash after picking up the second set, and as far as I know they just keep cycling round.'

'Well, we can't use large leaves as in the old myths,' Arki continued, 'as we haven't found any big enough.'

'You mean nature's been that generous!' Glyn responded, and the laughter rang out again, being the only sound apart from the muffled sound of their footsteps.

As the sun dipped towards the western horizon, the slanting rays lit up the area of fused sand nodules turning them into a myriad of twinkling stars, winking in and out of existence as the travellers walked along.

'It's surprising that such a beautiful sight could hold such a deadly threat to life,' said Arki with a sigh.

'I agree,' replied Glyn, stopping for a moment to look at the scintillating sands, 'at least we can now see the outline of the dangerous area, and that'll save us quite a bit of extra walking. I had intended going right to the end of this ridge, just to be sure of missing the radioactive area.'

They now turned at right angles to their old line of walking, and headed off down hill again, Glyn considering that if they kept going straight ahead, they would safely bypass the danger area by a small margin.

Holding the radiation monitor in his hand, he lead the way past the edge of the knobbly glass area, listening out for the slightest increase in the steady tick, tick, of the sensor.

A warm breeze drifted across the deadly area towards them, carrying with it a harsh dusty metallic smell, but as the monitor didn't warn them of any dangerous radioactivity, they carried on, oblivious to the microscopic particles they were ingesting into their lungs.

By the time they had cleared the danger area, the sun was only about two hours from disappearing below the horizon, and it was decided to seek out a suitable place to stop for the night.

The terrain was changing again, with smaller hillocks and deep gullies replacing the rolling slopes of the early afternoon, and it was in one of these that the first sign of life in that day's travel came to light.

A blob of grey green could be seen at the end of the gully they were travelling along, and this induced an increase of pace without a word being spoken.

As they neared the strange looking plant, it became obvious that no one recognized it as being anything like those they were used to on board the ship.

It stood alone at the end of the gully, surrounded by copious amounts of dead time whitened branches, the remains of those plants which hadn't quite made it in the dry and harsh environment in which they had tried to grow.

'Well, we've got some fire wood at least,' someone exclaimed, 'but who's going to gather it up with those spikes on it?'

The white gnarled and twisted branches were smothered in closely packed vicious thorns, some ten centimetres long, and with points as fine as any needle.

'I don't think we'll find a better place to make camp tonight, so let's clear an area over there of these prickly branches, and build a sheltering wall with our packs. It all came so naturally to Glyn.

Removing the dead plants wasn't quite so easy as had at first been assumed. Some still had deep roots attached, and although the wood was dead, it still had considerable strength.

One particular dead plant was right in the middle of the area they intended to sleep on, and despite all efforts, it remained stubbornly fixed in the ground. They had snapped all the thorns off using their feet, but two men pulling as hard as they could wouldn't free the plant from the firm hold it had in the ground.

Someone had the bright idea of digging the earth away from around the plant, and after much hacking away with a large flat stone, they had managed to make a small crater around the base, and then they saw why it was so firmly rooted to the spot.

Where the plant protruded from the stony ground, a network of thick roots spread out in all directions, some sideways and some directly downwards. There was more of the plant below ground than there was above.

Four of the biggest men grabbed hold of the naked stem and pulled in unison, but it still refused to come free, and they gave up the unequal struggle.

One of the fire makers of the previous night came forward and suggested that they burn it out of the ground, and as no one could think of a better idea, he set about rubbing his sticks together, which he had fortuitously saved.

It was several minutes later when a very hot and tired fire maker produced a small glowing bundle of tinder which he proceeded to blow on, encouraging it to burst into flame.

Once a few small twigs had caught fire, the process speeded up, larger twigs and handfuls of thorns being added to the small fire around the base of the plant.

The next event took them all by surprise. The main stem of the plant began to writhe about like a thing possessed, emitting squeaking noises amid the crackle of the general fire, and then the living bush, many metres away began to follow suit, the pair dancing and twisting like a pair of drunken ballet dancers.

Everyone backed away from the performing bushes, not knowing what else might happen.

'Must be connected by underground roots,' exclaimed Arki, 'and what one feels is experienced by the other.'

'But this one is dead, unless it's not as dead as we assumed,' one of the fire makers added.

There was a sudden gush of flames as a small oil storage nodule at the base of the main stem split open, expending in a few seconds the energy it had taken years to store.

Soon after that the fire died down, with just a few wisps of smoke drifting up into the still evening sky.

'Right,' said Glyn, 'let's gather up some of this loose dead wood and get a good fire going, we are going to need the heat later on, and the light will enable us to see what we are doing with the food packs.'

Everyone opened a food pack, adding the water they had saved from the last time they drank, and making up the difference from the emergency water supply, which was being used for the first time.

'Keep all empty containers,' Arki called out as the evening meal got under way, 'they will be useful for holding extra water, or whatever we might find to eat,' if we ever do he added under his breath.

After the meal, general conversation carried on for a while, but as everyone was exhausted after the gruelling march that day, they soon huddled down behind the wall of packs to get some sleep.

A few of the more fortunate ones had a sandy patch to lay on and were able to scoop out a depression for their hips, so ensuring a good night's rest. They were only disturbed once by a strange wailing noise which drifted across the gully, and then was gone. A vivid imagination kept a few awake for a while, and then all was quiet apart from the soft moaning of a light wind across the top of the hill.

Next morning they all seemed a bit more cheerful, as they were getting better adjusted to sleeping out in the open. There were a few requests for another ration of food, but as Glyn pointed out, they may be hungry but the previous night's ration would sustain them for twenty four hours.

After a limited drink from the emergency water supplies, they were off again.

The rising sun spread a pink glow over the tops of the surrounding hills, adding a fairyland touch to the scene and thereby disguising the true nature of the hostile land through which they were to travel.

'I could do with a good shower,' Arki commented to Glyn as they began the ascension out of the gully.

'Me to, and our clothes could do with a wash. The fine dust particles lodged in the material will cause it to wear before its time if we're not careful, so a bit of laundry is called for, at the earliest opportunity.'

The climb out of the gully was steep, and everyone was a little out of breath by the time they had reached the top, but fortunately the cool morning air had made the ascent a little more bearable.

The view from the hill top was a little more encouraging than the previous sightings of the distant green clad hills. They must have travelled a lot further than they thought, weaving in and out of the gullies the previous day. The plant growth could now be plainly discerned, with what looked like tall trees poking up out of the overall green mantle of the undulating ground ahead. On the far horizon, a jagged row of mountains poked their stark black sombre heads up into the clear blue sky of the early morning.

'There should be food of sorts somewhere in that mass of greenery,' Glyn said hopefully, 'and we'd better find it before our rations run too low.' Arki just nodded, he was transfixed at the sight of so much green after days of barren rock and sand.

They still had some distance to go before they would reach the green clad area, and the thought of what they might find spurred them on at an ever increasing rate, some actually breaking into a run at the bottom of the slope where it levelled out before the next rise.

What had looked like just another ordinary hill to climb from a distance, turned out to be something quite different when they reached it.

The first few steps up the slope brought everyone to an unintentional halt, their feet sinking further into the very fine sand with every step.

'I thought it was too good to be true,' moaned Brendon, who had lost his balance and was now sitting on the shifting sands, and slowly drifting down the slope.

Arki made one more attempt to climb the sand slope, and sank up to his knees in the fine dust.

'There's no way we can get up here,' he said, trying to extricate himself from the sucking effect of the sand.

The group assembled at the bottom of the slope, somewhat crestfallen, but not beaten.

'How about laying the packs in a line and crawling over them?' someone brightly suggested, with little conviction.

'It might be worth a try,' said Glyn, secretly doubting that it would work.

A line of backpacks were laid up the slope, but a soon as the weight of a person was added, the packs sank from view and for a few moments there was panic at the thought of the precious contents being lost for ever.

Eventually the packs were recovered, dusted off, and slung over tired shoulders.

'We'll have to go along the bottom of this sand slope until we find a way around it, or perhaps more stable sand which we can walk on.' Glyn sounded as fed up as the others looked.

They trudged on for what seemed like hours, stopping once for a drink, and then on again.

The valley between the long hill they had come down and the fine sand bank wound and twisted its way eastwards, taking them well off the southern course they had intended to follow.

Disgruntled comments were beginning to fly thick and fast, and Glyn was losing patience with those who moaned but could offer no solution to the problem.

He was about to call a halt and have it out with the malcontents once and for all, when they rounded a bend in the valley bottom and were confronted by a jumbled mass of broken rock.

'That's going to take a bit of climbing over,' said Arki, immediately adding 'but I'm sure we can do it.' in response to a withering look from Glyn.

Glyn and Arki moved forward, while the others having had enough marching for one day, tried to find a cool resting place in the shadow of the bend, and sat down.

'There's something odd about that rock,' Glyn stated, 'I've never seen a rock with a piece of metal sticking out of it.'

They moved closer and found other large lumps of what seemed to be rock, equally adorned with metallic rods protruding from their surfaces.

'It reminds me of something,' Glyn said, scratching his head and trying to recall something he had once read in one of the books a long time ago.

'Got it!' he exclaimed. 'Buildings were reinforced with metal rods to give them extra strength, and these blocks aren't rock, but concrete, an artificial building material made from something called cement, mixed with sand and gravel.

'This must have been a building, a bit like our ship, but standing on the surface. People lived in them, and factories for making things were put in them. Never thought I'd see one though.'

'I don't think we're seeing one now, just the remains after something rather powerful disassembled it,' Arki remarked, 'but interesting, just the same,' he added.

'Well, we can't go up the sand slope, the hill on our left is too steep at this point to climb safely and this jumble of broken building is blocking our way forward. We either have to go back to a point where we can climb the hillside, or find a way through this heap of rubble, the blocks are far to big to climb.' Glyn was trying to apply logic to the situation, but it didn't resolve the problem.

'There are some dark openings over there,' Arki pointed to a gap between several massive blocks, 'there might be a way through the pile, it's just possible,' he added.

Six:
Food and Drink

THEY SHED THEIR packs and approached one of the dark gaps at the base of the pile. Glyn entered first, cautiously, just in case there were holes in the ground which he couldn't see.

'Be careful not to disturb anything,' he called back to Arki.

'Anything likely to move would probably have done so by now, it has been like this for such a long time,' Arki replied, as they both worked their way deeper into the jumbled mass.

'I think we should wait here a while to let our eyes get accustomed to the low light level,' Glyn suggested, and they sat down in the gloom, wondering what they had got themselves into and if it was wise to proceed any further.

A little light filtered down from above, glancing off some of the smoother surfaces, and after a short time they could both see quite well.

'I think there's a faint breeze blowing through here, I can feel it on my face,' Arki observed, 'and that would explain why these gaps between the blocks haven't been filled with sand, it just blows straight through. Therefore, we should be able to get through.' He felt pleased with his reasoning..

'I think you're right, come on, let's give it a try.'

It was some time later when they broke out into daylight, and had to shield their eyes against the glare.

'Well done Arki, that was a shrewd observation on your part, so we should be able to get the others through.'

Backtracking through the rubble of the old ruin wasn't quite so easy, and they lost their way twice. Finally they made it back to the others, and broke the good news.

Some members of the group were none too happy about going into the remains of the old ruin, but as there wasn't an alternative, they gave in to Arki's cajoling and began the long struggle through.

Just before they had reached the other side of the ruin, Glyn and Arki inadvertently went downwards, having missed the original route they taken earlier. As they realized their mistake, someone called out that he had felt a wet rock, and that must mean there was water somewhere nearby.

Despite the almost dark conditions, the search for a possible water supply went ahead and almost ended in tragedy.

A startled yell echoed between the gaps in the broken concrete, followed by a loud splash. Someone had found the water the hard way.

Glyn wriggled his way through the others in the confined space between the blocks, and would have fallen in himself if it hadn't been for a restraining hand which grabbed his arm as he lost his balance at the edge of the drop to the pool in the old lift shaft.

Somewhere in the darkness below a frantic splashing and spluttered words could be heard.

'Don't panic,' Glyn called out, 'just tread water, help's on its way.' Instructing the man who had saved him from a similar fate to hold firmly onto his ankles, Glyn unhitched his pack in the confined space and lowered himself over the edge of the hole to reach down to the man struggling desperately in the water below.

Cold wet fingers clamped around his outstretched his hand in a vice like grip, and a voice gurgled 'Thanks, that was a close one.'

'See if you can climb up my body, use it as a rope,' Glyn grunted, as he struggled to breath in such an unnatural position.

The man climbed up Glyn's body, Glyn was hauled up from the lip of the shaft and all three of them crouched there in the near darkness, panting for breath.

'Did you swallow any of the water?' asked Glyn when he got his breath back.

'I'll say I did, must have been several litres. Come to think of it, it tasted quite good, but very cold.' he said, his teeth chattering as he spoke.

'Right,' said Glyn, 'let's get you up to the surface and dry you out. If you feel no ill effects from your enforced drink, we'll all have one and top up our supplies.'

It was some while later before everyone had crawled through the tumbled blocks and reached the outside of the ruined building, and having got out, no one was very keen to re-enter it to get water.

'The light will begin to fade soon, so we'll camp here for the night. We can shelter in the rock pile, as it should be a little warmer than out in the open.' Glyn was feeling his old self once more.

There was no fire that night as they sat around eating another emergency ration from the dwindling supplies, and Glyn told everyone to drink as much water a they liked, for tomorrow they would refill their containers.

'Well, at least one of us doesn't reek to high heaven any more, but I very much doubt if you'll get anyone else to take a bath down there.' Arki said with a grin. Glyn nodded his agreement, and then a vagrant twist of air wafted up from under his arm, and he nearly changed his mind.

As the sun went down and the heavens lit up with their usual sprinkle of star dust, discussions as to what the building might have been began.

Arki thought the building had been very wide and high because of the huge amount of rubble in the gully, and the water hole had probably been a lift shaft servicing the many levels below ground.

Speculation as to how far down the building had gone was anyone's guess, but the fact that the shaft hadn't filled up with sand over the many years since the disaster, suggested it went down a lot further than they liked to think about.

Next morning, when the sun had risen sufficiently for the light to filter down through the jumble of concrete blocks, they transferred the emergency water supplies from one container to another so that most were filled again, and the empty ones were taken down to the water shaft, the tallest member of the group reluctantly being held by the ankles over the lip of the hole to refill the empties.

The sun had now risen enough to warm everyone up, and it was a relatively cheerful band of travellers which set off along the gully, still looking for a way to go south again.

The soft sands which they were unable to climb earlier, suddenly took on a different appearance. It was now darker in colour and the grain size had increased to some extent.

'Let's try again,' said Glyn, turning right and up the slope. This time he didn't sink into the surface, and the others followed suit as soon as it was obvious that the sand would take their weight.

About half way up the slope, the radiation counter began to chirp away, warning of an increase in deadly rays well above the normal background level.

Glyn uttered a string of expletives which made Arki look up in wonder, and the pair of them came back down the slope as fast as they could, the others having already turned back towards the gully.

'If it's not one damn thing, it's another.' commented Glyn, the frustration of not being able to follow his chosen course south beginning to show for the first time.

'This gully is bound to end sometime.' said Arki, hopefully.

Just before they broke for the midday rest, the sand on their right levelled out and then disappeared to be replaced with small stones and gravel, and as the height of the mound was decreasing rapidly, they stayed on the gully floor as the walking was easier.

What caused more excitement than the disappearing sands, were the thin scattering of dead plant stems, which grew in frequency as they plodded along.

'At this rate we should hit green plants soon.' someone called out, and a little cheer went up to join the noise of the snapping twigs as they rounded a bend in the gully.

Before them a flat plain stretched out towards the green hills in the distance, the plain itself being dotted about with the odd grey green plant, the colour deepening into the distance indicating an increase of vegetation.

They all stopped to look at the first real greenery since leaving the ship and its hydroponics gardens.

'Don't expect to see familiar plants like those we had in the gardens, I think most of them were specially bred for our benefit.' said Glyn, not really sure if they were or not, but it was the easiest way to convince the others that they mustn't take anything for granted.

'Remember, don't eat anything without first checking it with me or Arki, it could make you very ill or even kill you.'

A murmur of acceptance rippled around the assembled group, but after the black berries, they were eager to try anything to supplement the emergency rations.

Looking up at the sun, Glyn made a few mental calculations and indicated what he thought was south, and they then headed off across the plain towards what they assumed to be some kind of forest, as something green was sticking up well above the other growth which carpeted the hills.

The further they went, the more numerous were the plants, although not all were alive and flourishing. Dotted among those still thriving were small groups of dead material, as if something had poisoned little areas of the plain, and the plants had succumbed to what ever it was after their initial growth.

So far, there were no signs of berries or other fruiting bodies, and this lack of an alternative food source was disappointing to everyone, especially Glyn and Arki, who wanted above all else to preserve some of the emergency rations in case of future problems.

What had at first appeared to be a flat featureless plain, turned out to be a series of gently undulating folds in the landscape, the plant growth being more populous in the shallow valleys, thus indicating that adequate water was only present at these lower levels.

At one point the plants were so close together that they had to force their way through them. All was going well until a scream rent the other wise still air. Brendon was clutching his leg and complaining bitterly about the thorn which had entered his calf muscle as he wriggled his way through a particularly dense bush.

'Why don't you walk in line like all the others?' queried Arki, 'then this sort of thing wouldn't happen to you.'

Glyn came over to see what all the fuss was about, and gave Brendon the standard hard look which he was so good at doing.

'I thought it might be you.' he said, looking at the thorn.

'Why do you always pick on me?' wailed Brendon.

'I'm not picking on you, but you're always getting into trouble, usually through doing something stupid.' The area around the thorn had gone a nasty deep purple colour.

'We'd better get it out,' said Glyn, 'before his leg drops off.' the look of horror on Brendon's face almost made Glyn feel sorry for him, but not quite.

A gentle pull, and then a twist and pull achieved little other than to make Brendon scream even louder than before.

'Oh do shut up,' exclaimed an irritated Glyn, 'don't be such a damned coward.'

'It's not your leg,' retorted Brendon indignantly, 'so how would know how much it hurts?'

'Arki, could you get me another thorn like this one?'

'What are you going to do?' asked Brendon, his eyes opening even wider.

'Stick one in the other leg, and then you'll have a matching pair.' retorted Glyn, and then he relented,

'I'm going to check the other thorn to see why this one doesn't want to come out, OK?'

'I suppose so.' replied Brendon, resignedly.

Arki returned with an identical thorn, handing it to Glyn.

'Be careful how you handle it, it's got the nastiest set of claws on it you could imagine.'

'Now that's clever,' said Glyn, 'they're very small, but set back at an angle, so any movement will pull the main thorn in still further. This implies that there must be something mobile around here to be attacked, apart from fatty here, as things like this don't develop in nature without a purpose.'

'That's a nasty thought.' said Arki, looking over his shoulder instinctively. 'Anyway, back to the thorn. I don't see how we can pull it out without taking half the leg muscle with it, so how about flexing the muscle over to one side and then pushing it straight through.'

Glyn pushed the calf muscle over to one side and looked at it for some moments.

'Yes, I think you're right, it's the only way we can do it.'

Turning to Brendon he said, 'Now this is going to hurt a bit, in fact quite a bit, but it is the only way we can get it out. If we leave it in you may lose your leg altogether as there seems to be some sort of poison involved here, so we are going to push it right through.'

Realizing they needed something to push the thorn with, Arki looked around for a small piece of stick about the same size as the thorn, and having found one, gave it to Glyn saying, 'You'll have to push it through to start with, and I'll grab it when it comes out the other side.'

They both looked at Brendon to see how he was taking it, and were relieved to see he had fainted clean away.

'Quick,' said Arki, 'now's your chance.' Glyn pulled the muscle over to one side, positioned the small stick on the end of the thorn and pushed.

It went in so easily that they were both surprised, but Arki failed to grab the sharp end as it emerged from Brendon's leg. He then shed his jacket, and folding the arm in two so increasing the material thickness, frantically clutched at the protruding thorn, and pulled it clear.

Glyn quickly took a mouthful of water from his container, applied his mouth to the wound and blew with all his might.

At first just a small trickle of water came out, and then a great gush along with some grey slimy substance. After several more applications of the water blowing, just blood and water came through, and then they pinched the wounds closed.

'It should clot fairly soon, and then it will take care of itself.' said Arki, hoping he was right, and that all the grey stuff was out. Brendon opened his eyes and looked down at his leg.

'It's all over now, no more pain, just a little soreness for a while.' Arki felt sorry for the wounded man, after all, he was one of nature's sad accidents, walking around just waiting for something to happen, and usually it did.

'Let that be an object lesson to all of you.' Glyn said to the others as they grouped around the still suffering Brendon. 'We don't know what we'll find here, so be on your guard all the time. Right, let's get on with the journey.'

In single file, they walked at a brisk pace with Glyn and Arki taking it in turns to lead, always on the lookout for the unexpected.

Each time they went up a gentle rise and down the other side, the plants grew in ever increasing profusion, some of them sporting flowers, until Glyn called a halt as it was now getting very difficult to push through some of the bushes, also the possibility of more thorn plants couldn't be ruled out, although none had been encountered so far.

'How about we go along the ridge, looking for a thinner patch of growth in the depression below, and then cross over?' Brendon had forgotten about his injured leg, and impressed them all with his logic.

'Now that's a very good idea, well done.' said Glyn, most surprised of all, and actually smiled at him.

The idea worked, although it did add a little extra length to the journey, but as they were getting nearer to their goal, they didn't seem to care too much about the extra steps taken. It was while they were crossing one of the depressions where there was a large gap in the plant growth and a little boggier, that the next surprise came. Glyn and Arki had gone across the soggy ground safely and turned to see if all was well with the others, when one of them almost sank out of sight, arms waving and yelling his head off.

They rushed to his aid, grabbing his arms as he began to sink out of sight. It took four of them to pull the unfortunate man up from the soggy mess of the bog, but what no one could understand at first was that they hadn't sunk, despite the fact that were so close to him when pulling him out.

As he finally emerged, black and slimy, a long grey tentacle was still wrapped around his legs, and was doing its best to pull him back down.

The sheer pulling power as more of the group joined in saved him, the grey tentacle finally losing its grip. It remained waving about in the air, trying to find its meal for a few moments, and then it slithered back into its hole in the boggy ground.

'Looks like we have a little more wildlife around here than we expected.' Arki remarked, as they all regained the safety of dry ground.

There was little they could do for the man who almost became a meal for something very unpleasant, except scrape off as much of the mud as possible, and try and console him with a drink of water.

'Whatever that thing was, it must have a large hole under the bog's surface and will grab anything which moves nearby.' Glyn stated the obvious as he couldn't think of anything else to say.

'Perhaps if we compromise, and cross any suspected area as close to large plants as possible instead of going for the clear patches.' Arki made it almost sound like a question.

'Well, it's certainly worth a try, but let's be extra careful.' replied Glyn.

They skirted the soggy area of the bog, keeping as close as possible to the plant life which grew around its edges and made it safely to the other side.

At the top of the next slope an area of what looked like grass spread out into the far distance, but not grass as they knew it. It was very short, dark grey green in colour and somewhat like a close cropped curly crew-cut, each little blade twisting around its neighbour, thus forming a close knit mat so that no sign of the underlying earth was seen.

'It's very pleasant to walk on, but what is it hiding underneath it?' someone asked of no one in particular.

Up until then, everyone had been enjoying the soft yielding springiness of the new terrain, but now a look of apprehension had overcome the group.

'Walk in the footsteps of those in front, I doubt you'll come to much harm.' said Glyn, striding out confidently.

'But what about you?' said Brendon solicitously, 'you're taking the first steps.'

'Goes with the job.' Glyn replied over his shoulder.

Arki smiled at Brendon's propitiatory attitude.

They marched on, and as nothing untoward had happened, Glyn increased the pace as he was anxious to reach the cover of the distant band of greenery. Being so exposed out in the open was beginning to make him feel a little uneasy, and he wanted to reach the cover of the trees before nightfall.

Travelling over terrain which all looks the same can be deceiving to the eye, as distances are difficult to judge accurately. And so it was for Glyn and his band of followers, the promised line of trees seemed to dance temptingly in the shimmering haze of the afternoon, but seemed no nearer, despite the forced pace of the march.

Glyn called a halt for a rest and a drink, carefully stamping on a circle of ground to make sure there were no surprises lurking underneath, and they all sat down, hot, weary and somewhat dispirited at their apparent lack of progress.

'What do you think we'll find when we get to the trees?' asked Brendon, anxious to keep in Glyn's good books after the praise he received from his suggestion earlier at the bog.

'I don't know really. I very much doubt if we'll find much that is the same as the plants we used to grow on the Ship, as I suspect they were genetically modified to best suit our needs. More than likely, the radiation released here has also modified all life forms but in an uncontrolled manner, and probably destroyed many species in the process. The greatest threat could come from predatory creatures, like the giant worm thing in the bog. I think we should devise some form of weaponry for our protection, although I don't know what we can make it from.' Arki looked worried at his own thoughts on the matter.

Just then Mia, who was sitting next to Glyn, gave a little cry. 'I felt it kick, do you think it's trying to get out?' she asked in a frightened voice.

'No, not yet,' said Glyn, 'I expect its shifting around trying to get comfortable, it must be very constricting in there.'

Mia rubbed her stomach thoughtfully, her partner was usually right about things, but a second movement of the baby caused some doubt in her mind as to whether he knew much about things maternal.

Arki was first on his feet, the others quickly following and the march was underway again, with Glyn in the lead as usual.

The first sign of the coming evening was a cool breeze which limped across the open plain in a half hearted fashion as if it wasn't sure which direction to take.

With the agreement of the others, Glyn increased the pace of their march, intending to reach the green belt of treelike growths before the light failed.

The short springy grass beneath their feet took on a different character as they progressed, the first change being the length of each blade and the lack of curl, more like the type of grass they were used to back in the ship.

Before long, the grass was almost up to their knees and impeding their progress. As well as the fact that it was beginning to take quite a fair amount of sheer physical effort just to push through it, Glyn was also being a little more careful about what might be hidden amongst it.

A few paces further on and the first flowers appeared. At this point they all stopped to admire the delicate blooms, the first show of real colour, apart from the dull green of what few plants they had seen and the equally uninspiring browns and greys of the arid landscape.

'No sign of any berries yet,' commented Arki wistfully, 'I could surely do with a good helping of something fruity.'

They looked around, but only unfamiliar seed pods could been seen dotted among the flowers, and no one was going to risk eating them.

'It looks as if there are some taller bush-like growths up ahead,' said Glyn, 'so we may be in luck after all.'

The first of the larger bushes they came to had no flowers or berries, just thin curled up leaves as if it was trying to conserve moisture by exposing as little of itself as possible.

Twenty metres further on and they were smiled upon by the Gods, a large bush of the black berry type they had raided a few days ago bore a large crop of juicy ripe fruits, and it wasn't long before the bush was stripped bare of its efforts to procreate by the hungry band of travellers.

'I would suggest no more than five or six berries each, remembering what happened last time.' suggested Glyn, but no one was listening to good advice at the moment.

With their lips and fingers stained purple and satisfied smiles on their faces, the group lined up behind Glyn without a word being spoken, and the trek continued southwards, everyone looking out for more of the delicious berries as they forced their way through the ever increasing height of the tall grass-like plants.

As the first of the small trees or large bushes appeared, but it was hard to tell which they were from this distance, the general topic of conversation was naturally on food. If the wooded area had berries and fruit, then one of their most urgent problems would be solved.

How many might succumb to poisons contained in the unfamiliar offerings didn't bear thinking about, so nobody did. If it hadn't been for Glyn's insistence that everything was checked out thoroughly, not many would have survived the first few days in their new home.

The undulations in the terrain grew steadily as the edge of the forested area approached, the final hump in the landscape revealed a deep gully with a ribbon of water trickling along it. If the water was drinkable, then that was another problem solved, and Glyn felt very pleased at the find.

'I'll go down first to check it out, the rest of you follow when I give the signal.'

He almost fell down the last few metres of the slope as it was covered in thin slate like debris on which a slippery mould had grown.

The water, when he reached it, was a smaller trickle than it had looked from above, and very shallow.

Looking up the gully, a series of large boulders lined the waterway, the meagre stream having cut its own path deep into the terrain in earlier times when rainfall had been much heavier.

'I'm going to work my way up to those rocks, you go along the top of the ridge and I'll call you down if there's a good crossing over point.'

By the time he had reached the rock pile, the others having a much easier journey along the ridge were showing some degree of excitement, and pointing down into the gully.

As he climbed over the last of the large rocks, he could see what all the fuss was about. A large pool of water stretched up the gully for some ten metres, and it looked quite deep.

Glyn bent to scoop some water into his hand, it seemed innocent enough with no plants growing in the water to hide any nasty surprises. It was sweet, no metallic aftertaste, and he looked up smiling, a thin trickle of water dribbling down his chin and staining his jacket with a dark wet patch.

'Come on down, but carefully, the water's fine so you can drink your fill.' The others scrambled down the steep slope, some in an undignified manner as they neared the water's edge and their feet met the first of the slippery stones.

When all had quenched their thirsts and replenished their water containers, it was a much more cheerful group which sat down at the water's edge to rest a while.

'If we can find a suitable place near here to make a permanent or semi-permanent camp, then it would be a good idea to wash our clothes, as well as take a much needed bath. Tomorrow, we could make a small dam up stream and use that to provide drinking water, and then this pool could be used for bathing and washing our clothes. Does anyone have any other ideas on the matter?' asked Glyn.

He looked around, and everyone seemed to be in agreement with what had been proposed, nodding their affirmation.

Things were getting better by the day, he thought.

'As we still have a good bit of daylight left, let's move on a little and see if we can find some fruit in the bushes or trees on the next ridge, we can always return here to make camp for the night, unless we find somewhere better.' Glyn had already begun to walk up the length of the pool to where it narrowed to a little stream so that he could cross over without getting his feet wet. The rest soon followed at the thought of finding something succulent to augment the emergency rations, which would be issued later.

Having reached the top of the next ridge, they found they were a little nearer to the trees than previously thought as the hollow below them was full of growth, which from a distance had appeared as another flat section of the landscape.

'Careful as you go down,' Glyn called out, 'we don't know what we'll find here.'

As they descended the slope, the undergrowth grew thicker and taller making the descent difficult in the extreme. So far there had been no bushes with the deadly spines or anything else to cause problems, apart from the actual density of the growth itself.

Reaching the bottom of the gully, they were all relieved to see tall slender trees reaching up into the sky above, a pale dappled light filtering down to illuminate the forest floor which was just bare ground, the light level being insufficient to sustain plant life.

The ground at this point seemed level, and went on into the far distance until it was blotted out by the sheer number of tree trunks.

'Not much to eat down here by the look of it.' someone commented acidly, when Arki, who had come down last said ,'Look up there, those look like apples, but much smaller than the ones we had back on the ship.'

Well out of their reach, several apple like fruits dangled from long thin branches, as if they had once been up amongst the tree tops, but the weight of the fruit as it grew had bent them down into the gloom below.

'How the hell can we get them down from up there? The tree trunk is far too thick to shake, and I doubt if anyone could climb up and reach them.' the same voice as before said gleefully.

'I don't think we're beaten yet,' said Glyn, eager to quash any doom mongers, 'there's a vine or creeper like thing spiralling up the trunk, if we can cut it off at the bottom and unwind it as it goes up until it reaches the thinner section, then we can shake the tree, maybe.'

Cutting the vine off at the point where it left the ground to begin its twisting climb to the light above seemed an impossible task, as no one had a blade or other means of cutting the tough looking growth.

'Someone will have to go back to the stream and fetch several thin flat stones. We may be able to hack our way through the stem with a bit of luck,' Glyn suggested, adding 'take someone with you, we must never go anywhere alone, under any circumstances.'

'I'll go.' Brendon volunteered, which surprised them all as it was a hard and difficult climb back up to the ridge top.

'I'll go with you.' Arki quickly added, more to make sure that Brendon returned in one piece than out of brotherly love.

The rest of the group stood around, some leaning against the tree trunks, waiting for the stone gatherers to return.

'Remember,' said Glyn loudly, 'no one is to try eating the fruit until we know for sure that it won't harm us, we have no means of coping with any poisonings, so be warned.'

A stony silence greeted his orders, as most had already built up images of biting into what looked like the sweet succulent fruits they were used to in the past.

A sudden crashing in the bushes at the edge of the trees announced the return of Brendon and Arki, carrying a selection of flat stones.

Selecting the sharpest edged stone, Glyn began energetically hacking away at the base of the vine, and soon a small pile of damp acid smelling white flakes littered the ground around the base of the tree.

As the remaining strand of the vine was severed and the vine pulled free from its base, Glyn noticed that his fingers were stinging and turning an ugly red colour.

'No one do anything until I'm back, I'm going to wash this juice from my hands, I think it's corrosive, so don't get any on yourselves.'

Having given his warning, he ran through the trees and up the bank to disappear into the mass of bushes which surrounded the forest, surprisingly followed by Brendon.

One of the group had moved forward and approached the severed end of the vine.

'Leave it, remember what Glyn said. Wait for him to return.' There was no doubt that Arki was accepted as second in command, as the man stopped dead in his tracks and said,

'I was only going to look at it. Just look at all that liquid running out of the end, how are we going to be able to keep that stuff off us if we have to handle the vine?'

'Let it drain away, it should all be gone by the time Glyn returns.'

Arki replied.

It was a very sick looking Glyn who staggered back through the bushes to the waiting fruit gatherers, and Arki rushed forward to help him before he fell to the ground.

'Remember, no one eats until we have tested the fruit.' Glyn called out as the small apple like fruits were eagerly gathered up by the rest of the group. Two men had taken their jackets off, and used them as carriers for the pile of fruit which was quickly growing at Glyn's feet.

'Who would like to act as fruit tester?' Glyn asked, thinking it unfair that Arki should do all the testing.

'I will,' a tall blond man stepped forward, 'it's about time I did something constructive.'

Taking one of the fruits, Glyn used one of the sharp edged stones to cut a small portion out.

'I'll squeeze a couple of drops of the juice under your tongue, if you feel dizzy or anything else untoward, let me know at once, and then spit out the remaining juice, OK?'

The man nodded, not looking so confident now that the test was about to take place.

'We'll go back to the water pool for the night, I think it'll be safer there. Gather up any dead branches or small pieces of wood on your way, we'll have a fire to cheer us up.' Glyn was already heading back towards the steep bank and the light of the open ground.

On the way back, someone discovered a small bush of black berries, and shortly after they had arrived back at the pool, the apple like fruit was declared safe to eat, the berries shared out and the fire maker had a good blaze going.

'One food pack between two,' Glyn called out, 'and don't eat too much fruit or the nutrient in the food pack will be long gone before you can extract the goodness from it.'

After the meal, they huddled around the blazing fire to keep the chill of the night air at bay, talking about what had happened in so short a time and speculating on what else they might find in the coming days.

Seven:
The Raft

THE DAWN WAS cooler than any they had experienced so far, and the sun was obscured by a dark ribbon of cloud which grew darker and thicker as they watched.

A sense of unease was felt by the group as they ate the rest of the fruit left over from the night before, and they looked to Glyn and Arki for reassurance. Deciding that doing something would probably settle everyone down again, Glyn suggested that they create a small pool up stream from the large pool, and use it for drinking purposes only.

Two volunteers were called for to go further up stream, walking on the ridge to see where the forest ended, as Glyn still wanted to go south and the forest looked too dense and dark to travel in easily.

By the time the upper drinking water pool had been constructed and filled with clear water, the two explorers had returned in great excitement.

'We've found another of those things you called a building, only this one seems to be nearly intact. It is divided into sections like our cabins, only much larger, and there is plenty of space for all of us to shelter in at night.' The bringer of the good news was a little out of breath as the pair had run all the way back from their find.

'Fill up all water containers,' Glyn called out, 'and we'll see what they've found.'

At last the building came into view, a creeper covered concrete block set into the bank of the gully, only its symmetry making it stand out from the surrounding lush greenery. It took longer to clamber down the steep and slippery bank and then cross the marshy area at the bottom of the gully, whilst watching out for any hidden perils which might lurk beneath the surface of the squishy ground.

The access to the building was set a few metres up the opposite bank, and the two discoverers proudly went ahead to show off their find.

A roughly oblong hole, only a metre high although it was a good deal wider, in the wall of the concrete structure seemed to be the only visible way in from the bank, and Glyn and Arki followed the other two into the dark chamber within the block, finding that they could stand up, and even with outstretched arms couldn't reach the ceiling above.

'Looks like we have found a new home.' said Arki, his voice sounding strange as it echoed back and forth from the solid concrete walls.

'Certainly looks that way,' rejoined Glyn, 'but remember it is only for a short time, as we must press on southwards, according to our instructions.'

They returned to the bright light of the outside world, shielding their eyes from the glare, although the sun wasn't visible as the cloud bank had thickened and spread half-way across the sky.

'I think the entrance has got silted up,' said Arki, 'how about digging it clear so that we can get in a little easier, and it will allow a bit more light in as well.'

Willing hands soon found flat sheets of slate from the opposite bank, and the clearing of the entrance began. It soon became apparent that the room behind the opening was also filled with debris, as what they assumed to be the doorway was now just over two metres high.

It was hard work, but with the group working in teams of two, one each side of the opening, cutting and passing the loosened debris from one pair to the next, they made surprising inroads into the room, whilst the debris formed an access ramp to the building on the outside.

By midday, although it was difficult to tell if it really was because the sun was now totally obscured by the cloud bank, they had cleared enough space in the first of the interconnecting rooms for all of the group to shelter come nightfall, and they still had the afternoon to go.

Arki suggested they should go looking for ferns or something soft to sleep on, as the concrete floor of the room was even harder than the ground of the previous night.

Two men and their partners came forward when they heard the suggestion, and were sent off to get bedding for the rest of the diggers who would surely need it come sleep time.

As the light began to fade, heralding the coming night, the room had been cleared of the accumulations of the passing years and some ingenious soul had made a crude broom of fine twigs to sweep it really clean.

It still had the dank smell of rotting leaves, but they would at least be sheltered from the cold winds of the night, and no one was going to quarrel with that.

At no one's bidding, the apple fruit and black berries had been replenished with enough for another feast at the early morning meal, and a pile of fire wood was growing at the entrance to their new home.

Once the fire had been started, Brendon came forward with a long bunch of fine twigs bound tightly together into a bundle, with a thick stick protruding from one end.

'What have you got there?' asked Arki, thinking it was another broom.

'If I light the end, it should burn for quite a time, and I can see the inside of the room which I haven't seen yet as I was on the outside clearing the stuff the others were throwing out,' he rushed it all out in one continuous stream, only pausing for breath to add, 'please.'

'What do you think, Glyn?' asked Arki, being careful to give their natural leader the right of veto.

'Don't see why not. Good idea of yours.' Glyn replied, placing a hand on Brendon's shoulder and giving him a pat.

He grew at least three centimetres in height as he unbent from lighting his firebrand, and beamed at the leader and his aide.

The three of them trooped into the gloom of the concrete chamber, Brendon proudly leading the way. Once inside, they were all surprised at the space the flickering firebrand illuminated, and as the others crowded in, shadowy shapes began to dance weirdly around the walls, much to the delight of the younger ones.

Brendon had gone over to the far corner of the room and it was Arki who first noticed that the smoke from the firebrand was going somewhere other than up to the ceiling, as only a small amount of it hung there.

'What's that above your head?' Arki asked, and Brendon raised his burning bundle of twigs as high as he could to reveal a small dark opening in the ceiling. The smoke was being drawn upwards and out of sight.

'Where's it going?' asked Glyn, a puzzled look on his face, 'there's only the concrete roof and a covering of creepers above us.'

One of the men nearest the entrance went outside and down the new ramp they had constructed to see where the mysteriously disappearing smoke was coming out of the building.

'No sign of it outside, at least none that I can see.'

'Well, it's got to go somewhere, perhaps we can trace it better tomorrow in daylight. At least it's cleared the air of that damp mouldy smell.' Arki added hurriedly, keen to get the evening meal underway.

Feeling he was on a roll, Brendon turned to Glyn saying,

'Perhaps we could have the fire in here, so we can get all the warmth from it, as the smoke seems quite happy to go up there.' pointing to the hole in the ceiling.

'You really are in good form today.' Glyn answered with a wide grin, and giving him another pat on the shoulder gave instruction for the firewood to be brought in, and a new fire to be lit in the corner of the underground room.

Someone had the sense to build a low stone wall around the burning sticks, so containing the fire and preventing the nearby bedding from joining the wood in its merry blaze.

The gathering clouds had completed their job of blotting out the lowering sun, and complete darkness soon followed, except for the concrete room and its occupants, bathed in the warm glow from the fire in the corner.

There was just enough light to enable the group around the fire to add the correct amount of water to their food concentrates, and the meal was finished with the most welcome fruit and berries gathered earlier.

Despite the hard work done during the day, no one seemed too keen to go to sleep, except the younger members, and the conversation went on long into the night, debating the reasons for their presence there and the possible outcome of moving on towards the equator, as the instructions had indicated they should do.

It was only when the main supply of wood had run low, and a small token fire kept going to keep the chill of night at bay, that everyone finally lay down to sleep.

In the early hours of the morning, a crackling explosion and a blinding flash of light woke everyone up. The moving storm which had been long brewing, finally found a suitable section of the landscape to vent its fury on, and did so.

The fire keeper immediately added a few small sticks to the glowing embers of the fire and blew on them, the tiny flames soon growing in size so that the walls were adorned by the ghostly dancing shadows of those moving around, trying to get their turn at the doorway to see the brilliant lightning display outside.

The rain must have been falling for some considerable time as the gentle trickle of water in the gully was now a raging torrent, tearing away at the banks, and it had already removed half the ramp which had been built yesterday from the debris of the sleeping chamber.

'Don't go onto the ramp,' Glyn yelled out over the thunderous cacophony of the storm, 'it won't take a lot to set the rest of it moving.' And with that the rest of the ramp gently slid down the slope to be swallowed up by the dirty crested thrashing waters which now nearly filled the gully, and if the rain kept up, would soon reach the doorway of their shelter.

The totally black sky was continuously riven by the snaking blue, white, and pink ribbons of lightning, streaking from cloud to cloud and from cloud to ground, one nearby strike throwing up a huge column of mud as it dissipated its energy into the earth in one furious millisecond.

Slowly the storm abated, but the rain continued to cascade down, filling the gully almost up to the entrance level of their shelter, and Glyn was beginning to get worried.

Should he move everyone out to higher ground and risk getting their supplies wet and ruined, or just sit the storm out and stand the chance of being washed away if the torrent in the gully suddenly surged and entered their chamber? Arki was just as undecided as he was, and so they stayed.

At last the rain eased to a gentle drizzle, and the noise of the storm seemed strangely distant and divorced from their surroundings, almost as if it were happening somewhere else and they were watching a visual recording of it.

Glyn and Arki, along with several others, were in the doorway of their shelter, when on the horizon a thin pale blue streamer of light leapt up from the ground and into the overhead clouds. Instantaneously, a massive purple tongue of lightning streaked downwards towards the ground, lighting up the surrounding land as if the sun had suddenly come out.

As the lightning strike died out, it was replaced by the biggest flash of light they had yet seen as a colossal yellow and red fireball headed skywards, the vivid fires within it twisting and churning as if they were alive.

'Quick, inside and lie down!' Glyn yelled out with an edge of panic in his voice.

As they threw themselves down onto the bedding, and the others followed suit, the pressure wave hit making their eardrums pop.

The blast of sound which followed left several of them who had been in direct line with it through the doorway, slightly deaf for a couple of days.

The ground heaved up and down several times, and the sound of the tormented earth trying to adjust to the massive pressures put upon it added a new sound and element of fear to that which had already overwhelmed them.

As the distant rumble of rock torn from the earth returning to its place of origin died away, the fire maker scraped together the glowing coals of his fire, added a few more sticks, blew on them nervously, and the chamber with its traumatized occupants was lit once more in a gentle glow.

'What do you think that was?' asked Glyn, not really expecting a sensible answer from anyone.

'Well, I think it was an atomic explosion, the fireball and the concussion wave certainly fitted the description I once read about in one of the books, and I can't think of anything else which would release that much energy in one go.' Arki quietly said to Glyn.

'But atomics haven't been used here for hundreds or maybe thousands of years, if we are to believe what we read when we opened the survival packs.' Glyn retorted, not at all convinced.

'Maybe so, but if there was an underground atomic power station, or a secret dump of atomic missiles buried deep within the earth, that lightning strike could have been just powerful enough to have started a chain reaction, and boom, up she went.' Arki spoke with such conviction that Glyn had little choice other than to believe him, especially as he couldn't think of a better answer.

'What about the radiation, do you think we got hit by that as well?' asked Glyn, bearing in mind the damage it could do to the project.

'I expect we got some, but the walls of this place are quite thick, and that must have stopped most of it.'

'Well there's nothing we can do about it now, but in future we must try and keep any exposure to radiation to the lowest amount possible, otherwise our genes, will be damaged, and the whole project will have been a huge waste of time and effort. I don't quite understand how it works,' Glyn added, 'but that is the gist of it according to what I've read.'

Next morning the clouds rolled away, as a grey cold dawn broke it seemed as if the earth itself was feeling miserable.

When it was light enough, Glyn went outside to survey the damage the storm had done. The gully was now nearly a metre deeper, and the rock dam they had so carefully built together with the larger natural one downstream, had been swept away. The stream still ran, chuckling and gurgling over a new obstacle course of rocks uncovered by last night's torrent, but not really fit for drinking as it still bore a considerable amount of silt.

'I would think by midday the water will have cleared enough for us to use it, so you can all drink your fill from the water containers and we'll refill them later.' Glyn announced hopefully.

They had a little fruit left over from the night before, and this was shared out as evenly as possible, the children being given the major portions.

'Do you think we should head south again?' asked Arki, as they trooped outside into the rather thin sunshine which was still trying to break through the few remaining clouds.

'Not just yet. We must replenish our water supplies first, and then it would be a good idea to see if we can find any more edible fruits in the forest so that we can recognize them more easily in the future. Also it's about time we found out what else we have in our survival packs, there was some mention of tools, I think.' Glyn was looking for a flat dry piece of ground on which to assemble his band of followers so that they could undo their backpacks, but the ground was still sodden after the night's torrential downpour.

While the sun was left to evaporate the last of the rain, it was decided to check out the nearby forest for more fruits, and after much searching in the soggy woods behind the ridge where the apples had been found the previous day, they were able to add a nut to their meagre food supplies.

It was like no other nut which Glyn or Arki had ever seen before, either in the ship or the books they had read, but Arki had a gut feeling that it was edible, and after the usual tasting trial, pronounced it fit to eat.

It was nearly as big as the apples they had found yesterday, and once the outer husk had been removed, proved to be a good source of protein, although a little indigestible if eaten in large quantities, as they found out later.

By the afternoon, the ground had dried out, and Glyn called everyone out into the open to search through their survival packs for anything useful, other than the food concentrates.

Soon they discovered that they had two light making devices, which when the button was pressed on one end, a beam of light emerged from the other. A warning message stated that the light should only be used in an emergency, as the power source was of limited ability.

A series of knife blades, which folded into their handles for safety, were greeted with the kind of enthusiasm reserved for chefs' special efforts, when it got it right, that is.

A pack of water purifying tablets, a flame provider for initiating fire, and a range of pills for various illnesses which none of them had ever heard of, let alone able to diagnose, made up the main itinerary of things which would help them stay alive in their new environment, or so thought the providers of the items.

One of the group found a large pack of something he couldn't open, so tightly was it wrapped, and gave it to Glyn for his appraisal.

Using one of the new found knives, he managed to carefully remove the multi layered waterproof wrappers, revealing a small handgun and several ammunition packs, also individually wrapped against the atmosphere.

Glyn held up the instruction sheet which came with the pack, and read aloud to the assembled group.

'This device is used to propel a metallic projectile at high velocity, the object being to kill or severely wound the target at which the device is pointed. You will not have had any knowledge of such a device before, so it is deemed expedient that the following directions be fully understood before the device is used,' Glyn read on, mouthing the words to himself as he saw little point in reciting the whole thing to the others, who would probably have forgotten most of it long before the device was needed.

Several other little items of interest were found, a ball of very tough twine, a small pack of plastic sheets and a pen like device with which to write on them, and a ball of what looked like clear glass.

This last item brought forth many ribald comments from those who had perfected that art long ago on board the Ship at the Chefs expense, not that the Chef had cared one jot.

A stock of apples, several large handfuls of the black berries and copious amounts of the new nuts had been retrieved from the forest by nightfall, and the usual shared pack of concentrates were now split among three people, the native foods being used to fill up the otherwise nearly empty stomachs.

The firewood stocks had been doubled so that a good fire could be kept burning all night if need be, and the stream was beginning to clear as they all retired to the concrete chamber in the side of the ridge for the night.

The night was quiet and uneventful as far as the people in the shelter were concerned, and a good night's sleep saw them fresh and eager to get on with the new day when it eventually dawned, bright and clear.

After their breakfast of fruit and nuts, Glyn suggested that they all washed their clothes and took a good bath in a pool formed by the storm.

Some stripped off without a care and ran down to the water's edge, much to the embarrassment of those of a more delicate nature, who, after a time, were cajoled by Arki to join the others as they didn't have anything to show which was different to those already in the water. Eventually, everyone had partaken of the waters, and clothes lay strewn about on sticks, rocks and anything else which would support them from the now dusty ground.

When everyone was dressed again, and the blushes had disappeared, Glyn suggested that they raid the forest once more for food stocks, as on the morrow they would be heading south again, as directed by the instruction sheet.

The strange disappearance of the smoke from their fire in the corner of the concrete chamber still held a fascination for Arki, who didn't like insolvable mysteries. He had checked outside to see where the smoke was coming out, and it wasn't. The top of the building was, as far as they could tell, just a solid block of concrete and there were no holes in it.

Not only that, it was covered in a thick layer of earth and a mat of creepers which over the years had interwoven to form an impenetrable barrier to smoke and man.

Arki reasoned there must be a draft which sucked the smoke to some outlet which they couldn't find and had to leave it at that, much to his disappointment.

Early next morning the group set off along the top of the ridge, following the stream towards its possible source, thus maintaining a supply of drinking water while trying to locate the edge of the forest so that they could turn south again.

It was two tiring days later, after leaving the ridge and travelling over a smooth rising plain of gravel which ended in a rocky ridge, that they were confronted by a view which brought a gasp from one and all, and they saw the next barrier in their progress south.

Ahead of them a vast expanse of water slowly drifted by. For as far as they could see, they were surrounded by forests on all sides except the one they had come from, and with the river dividing the land in two in a north south direction.

'We can't go back now.' Arki quietly said in an aside to Glyn, who was looking as shattered at the prospect of returning as Arki sounded.

'I know, but what can we do? There's no way around the forest, you can see it covering the hills right into the far distance on either side of this plain, and even if we could swim the river, which I very much doubt, we would only have more forest on the other side. It comes right down to the water's edge over there as it does here.'

They went down the gravel slope to the water's edge and made camp, although there was plenty of daylight left, they had nowhere to go.

'We've got to do something, so let's make up a small team and go see what the forest has to offer, it may not be as thick as it looks, and in that case we could go along almost at the water's edge perhaps.' Arki wasn't one for standing still. 'Good idea,' said Glyn, 'we'll stock up on fruit and berries at the same time, there can't be much left to eat except the concentrates.'

Six volunteers jauntily set off south, heading for the forest's edge in a business like manner, mainly to show those remaining that all was under control and partly to convince themselves that it was so.

The first few low bushes were a welcome sight, for many bore the black berries they had all enjoyed earlier, but it was obvious there was no possibility of travelling through the forest for any great distance, as the density of the undergrowth increased as they went further in.

'How come we have all this undergrowth here, when there wasn't any in the other forest where we got the apples?' Glyn asked Arki as they struggled to break through the mat of vines which hung down from the trees.

'Different conditions, I would think.' he replied, hoping that Glyn wouldn't ask him to expand on the matter as he couldn't see what the different conditions were.

'Well at least we have food here, and there are some new varieties to try by the look of it.' Glyn was looking up at a large plum like fruit, tantalizingly just out of his reach.

They turned left, hoping to reach the water's edge to see if progress would be any easier there, when the first of the dead trees came into sight. It seemed dead, as there were no green leaves on it, and the wood had a hollow ring to it when struck.

'If we had enough of these we could make a floating platform and drift south, as that's the direction the river is going in.' Arki observed. 'How could we hold them together?' asked Glyn, a faint ray of hope beginning to dawn.

'Use these creepers, they seem tough enough.' replied Arki, bending the thin end of one in his hands.

They tramped on, or to be more accurate, forced their way through the least thick undergrowth they could find in the direction they wanted to go.

Before they reached the water's edge, they came across several more fallen trees, and some dead but still standing.

Arki had begun to count them up as they went along.

Finally they broke out of the forest and nearly fell into the slow moving river, as there was hardly a dividing line between the two.

'Right,' said Glyn, having made his mind up as to what should happen next, 'let's collect as much fruit as we can and return to the others, then send another party out to collect some more.'

When they got back, the next team of gatherers were sent out while the new blue plum fruit was tested for safety. As luck would have it, it passed with flying colours, being sweet and filling, and so providing plenty of energy and the feeling of a full stomach, which would be welcomed by everyone. A smaller yellow version of the plum fruit was also tried, but spat out by the tester as being disgusting, poisonous or not. Later that evening around the camp fire, Arki explained his theory of making a floating platform to take them south.

Once the question of binding the logs together was explained, and the fact that one log would support two people in his estimation, there was little argument against the proposal, at least none which would hold up to close scrutiny.

Next day the log hauling began. It wasn't as difficult as they had first thought, as there were sixteen strong men and women in the group who applied themselves willingly to the task, and by nightfall, they had enough logs at the water's edge to build a raft big enough to carry them all, and room to spare for their provisions.

Early next morning the first log was rolled into the river, with a long vine attached to each end, the vines firmly attached to a stake driven into the shore.

As more logs were added and lashed to the preceding ones, the anchor vines were paid out, so allowing the raft to grow and still remain under control.

Arki realized that some form of protection from the sun would be a good idea, as a lot of light would be reflected off the water and sunburn could be a problem. Four uprights were driven into the raft and a simple framework constructed overhead so that it could be covered with broad leaves from the forest. Someone else suggested a side panel which could be moved to whichever side needed to be covered, completing the sun screening.

That evening, as the sun was sinking in the West, the raft was finished off, a good stock of fruit and nuts collected, and everyone felt very pleased with themselves. One enterprising fellow had made a quantity of long pointed staves, 'To fend off anything in the water which might take a fancy to us.' Glyn praised his ingenuity and thoughtfulness, and the staves were safely lashed to one of the centre logs.

Six long poles were cut for manoeuvring the raft in what they hoped would be shallow water, their intention being to drift along close to the edge of the river bank whenever possible, so that land could be reached in an emergency.

Brendon had the bright idea of putting some flat slates on one end of the raft so that they could have a small fire if need be. Glyn couldn't see why they would need a fire on the raft, but agreed to it as he didn't want to dampen any other good ideas which might be forthcoming.

That night they all ate and drank their fill around the biggest fire they had yet made, a few songs were sung, jokes were told by those of the company who usually kept their wit for berating the mechanical Chef, and a good time was had by all.

Not everyone slept too well that night, whether it was the excitement of the journey planned for next day or an over indulgence in the new plum fruit, was anyone's guess. Suffice it to say, there were a few bleary eyes next morning.

A quick meal in the grey chill air of early dawn saw everyone ready for the great adventure, this was something totally new in their experience, and one or two had doubts about the safety of the whole idea at the last moment.

But it was too late for doubts, Glyn was determined to go south, and the river was the only route available.

Everything was loaded onto the raft and lashed down with thin vines, the food stocks being piled up under the covered section along with the survival packs.

Glyn gave the word and they all clambered aboard, the raft dipping a little as the weight of the group concentrated on the front end.

'Spread yourselves around a bit,' he called out, 'we don't want to tip the whole thing up.' He needn't have worried, the raft would have taken twice their number and still floated, Arki had got his calculations wrong, luckily in their favour.

The tethering vines were released from the staves they had driven into the river bank, but the raft refused to move. They tried pushing with the poles, but to no avail, until someone realized the extra weight of the passengers had driven the rear end of the raft into the soft sand.

'OK, everyone up to the front end.' called Arki. Someone mumbled 'That's where we were in the first place,' and the raft floated free, turning down river as the strong current caught the front end.

'Use the poles to try and keep the raft just a few metres from the bank,' Glyn called out as they gathered speed, 'we don't know how deep it is further out, and we may lose control.'

By full sun-up they had drifted a considerable distance downstream, the river banks ever changing their contours, with small inlets where other streams joined the mighty flow.

The forest came right down to the water's edge in most places, and Glyn then knew that the river really was the only way open to them for southerly travel.

When the sun had reached its zenith, he calculated they were still heading south, the waterway holding a straight line through the landscape. But it was getting wider, and that could mean that it was also getting shallow, and the raft might get stuck on a ridge in the river bed.

'Two volunteers please, one each side of the front end. Mark a pole by scratching the bark off at about two metres from the end, and check the depth as we go along. If it is less than your mark, pole the raft out into the middle until you get the two metre level again.' Glyn was taking no chances of floundering on some vagrant mud bank, as the chances of getting it off again didn't bear thinking about.

Towards late afternoon, Arki noticed that raft travel was beginning to lose some of its novelty for those with nothing to do, as volunteers for the depth gauging at the front end were getting ever more persistent that it was their turn to take the poles.

A quiet word with Glyn, and it was decided to pull in at the next suitable place on the river bank for the night. They would need to replenish their food supplies and find fresh water from a stream, as the river water was a little murky and would only be used as a last resort. A deep inlet with a shingle bank caught Arki's eye, and the raft was turned in towards it using the poles.

The weight of the floating platform drove it some way up the gently sloping shingle bank, the clatter and rattle of the stones adding a welcome noise to the silence they had experienced all day, apart from their own voices and the constant lapping of the wavelets as they caressed the raft.

The mooring vines were made fast, holding the raft safely in place on the stony beach, and everyone enjoyed the freedom of stretching their legs, the younger ones racing up and down the shingle bank and shouting with joy.

The group split up, some gathering wood for the evening fire, others going into the nearby forest for fruit, while two men went up the little stream which had threaded its way through the stone mounds to join the river.

The sun dipped towards the far horizon, lighting up the forest in a pink glow and the fire was crackling away merrily, adding its warmth to the sudden chill air which had swept up the river and into the inlet.

All had returned from their foraging and were waiting for the evening meal, except for two who had gone up the stream, and Glyn was beginning to get a little worried at their absence.

'Better go see what's happened to them.' He said to no one in particular, when they came racing over the shingle bank amid a clatter of stones and in great excitement.

'Look what we've found.' said one, holding up a piece of shiny metal. It was about half a metre long, fifteen centimetres wide and two thick, and the reddening sunlight sparkled from it as he waved it about.

Everyone crowded around to see the artefact from a long bygone age, speculating as to what it might have been, and wanting to hold it as if doing so would connect them to those who had gone before.

'It would make a great cutting tool if we could only thin one edge down a bit, and sharpen it.' Arki said, visualizing a powerful hacking blade.

'I seem to remember,' he added, 'something about heating metal to reform it, read it in one of the old books.'

'What's a book?' someone asked, but no one bothered to enlighten him.

'We have fire, but I don't know if it would be hot enough to soften the metal, it must be very strong not to have corroded away after all this time,' Glyn said, 'but we could try, we've nothing to lose except a little time, and we've plenty of that.'

It was jointly decided that next day they would make a big fire and try to reform the strip of metal into a cutting tool, grinding the edge sharp on a stone.

No new fruits had been discovered by the foraging party in the forest, but a plentiful supply of those they had eaten before were collected. Glyn was keen to see if their digestive systems would tolerate a fruit and nut diet without the emergency rations, as these were going down at an alarming rate, so he suggested that they try it for one meal.

By next morning only two people complained of an emergency visit to the bushes during the night, but couldn't be sure that the fruit diet was totally responsible.

Brendon suggested a chimney be constructed to increase the draw on the fire, but when asked how that would work he didn't know, and looked sufficiently crestfallen at the query for Glyn to give the go ahead and build one.

It was only a metre and a half high, and constructed of rock brought from behind the pebble bank, but it certainly made a difference to the roar of the flames as they raced up the hollow space to belch forth in a fountain of smoke and sparks at the top.

It took a moment for Arki to realize that the embers at the bottom of the fire were the hottest part, and the stainless steel strip, not that they knew it as such, was then pushed into the glowing mass and soon began to glow bright red.

Eight:
Trial by Water

Two PIECES OF wood which had been cut flat and wound with a thin vine loop around them, formed an insulating handle to grip the heated metal when they withdrew it from the fire, although the end soon charred into a black and smelly mess.

The first few attempts at flattening the edge of the steel strip were a dismal failure, but persistent pounding with a large smooth stone and re-heating the steel paid off in the end, and Arki had the basic shape of his blade.

Someone had thoughtfully shaped a wooden handle for the new edition to their armoury, being two carved pieces of wood which they could bind together around the blade with thin creeper strands. It now only remained to sharpen the edge, and a hunt for the right kind of stone was under way.

Several different types of pebble were tried, and a fine grained flint like stone proved to be the best available. It was going to be a long and laborious job honing the edge, but Arki thought it would keep himself and several people occupied in turn on the next trip down river.

That night they kept the fire going in the chimney and tried baking some of the nuts on the hot stones. This made them much more palatable, and soon the remaining stock of nuts had been cooked and put on one side for the next day.

Baking the plum fruit didn't work very well, the juice running down the side of the chimney had charred leaving a sharp burnt sugar smell in the air, and that was when they saw their first insect.

The body was about fifteen centimetres long and thicker than a finger, two sets of translucent wings beat at such a high speed that they were almost invisible, filling the air with a deep humming noise as the creature darted about.

It seemed harmless and a pretty thing as it hovered over the head of one and then another of the assembled group, the firelight reflecting off its almost invisible gossamer wings in a myriad of iridescent colours.

Brendon thought the burning sugar from the plum fruit had attracted it to their fire, but the general consensus of opinion was the light from the fire itself had drawn it to them.

After a while it flew away, and they were sorry to see it go as it was the only pleasant living and moving thing they had seen since leaving the ship.

They settled down for the night, and in the early hours of the morning something in the forest screeched in agony several times, and was then silent. Not many slept after that, and morning couldn't come too soon.

After a quick meal, the raft was loaded up and they set off down river again, the current pulling the loaded raft out towards the centre, so a lot of work with the poles was needed to keep the floating log mass close to the shore.

Arki had begun to grind away the edge of his cutting blade, but it was very slow work and the blade had to be dipped frequently into the river, the water acting as a lubricant for the honing stone, but by keeping an eye out for the first signs of boredom among the travellers on the raft, he soon hoped to have some help with his blade forming.

By midday Arki had persuaded two others to help him with the blade grinding, and it wasn't long before they could see some reward for their hard work. The first few centimetres of the blade was now honed down to a fine edge, and Arki demonstrated its cutting effect by slashing at one of the logs, cutting a great chip out of the wet timber which then flew over the heads of the onlookers with a buzzing sound as it spun in the air.

Once the object of the exercise was fully understood, Arki had many willing hands to help him with the blade, taking it in turns to grind away at the hard metal.

Glyn checked their direction at midday by the sun and found that they were still going due south, and although many kilometres had been travelled there had been no bend in the river as yet which he would have expected considering the distance they had gone, and as far as he could see, it carried on straight to the horizon.

'Recalling pictures from the old books, rivers twisted and turned all over the place,' he said to Arki, 'and even on the maps of the earth, they were never in straight lines like this one. Can you account for it?'

'Can't say I can really. It maybe due to a long fault in the earth's crust, or something the others did before they blew the whole place up. It's anyone's guess as far as I can see.'

Just then, their attention was taken by a low dark smudge on the horizon, seemingly in the middle of the river. At that moment the two men with their depth poles called out that the water was getting shallow, with only a metre and a bit beneath the raft.

Glyn gave orders to pole out into the main stream until they had a clear two metres of water under them, and this they did, but it meant going nearly into the middle of the main flow to achieve it.

The raft picked up speed in the deeper channel and the blob on the horizon grew in size as they watched.

'At the moment we are heading straight for it, whatever it is,' said Arki, 'so do we bypass it or try for a landing to see what it is?'

'Let's go for a landing, we don't get much excitement just going down the river.' Glyn replied.

The island was fairly rushing towards them now, and it took all their skill not to get swept past it as the waters divided and accelerated around each side.

The raft finally ran up a shallow beach, jamming the forward logs firmly into the soft sand, and throwing three of its occupants off. The others had seen what was coming, and had braced themselves against the landing, although some left the raft in a slightly undignified manner as they lost their balance at the moment of impact.

Towering over them were the remains of a massive structure which at one time must have reached high into the brilliant blue sky above, but now there was only the broken stump to remind them of man's once mighty achievements.

'Do you think this was a building of some sort, like the one we left after the storm?' asked Arki, gazing up at the crumpled remains.

'Could well be,' replied Glyn, 'but this one was much bigger, in fact it must have been enormous, just look at the width of the base, it must have been even bigger than our ship and the complex which held it.'

Tell-tale brown stains on the huge concrete blocks told of enormous steel girders which had once held the building together, but something even mightier had descended from the skies and delivered a stunning blow to the structure, reducing it to a jumbled heap.

'I'd like to explore it, if we have the time.' Arki stated, and Glyn agreed, his curiosity also aroused by the sheer size of the remains. Stakes were driven into the beach to secure the raft, despite the fact that the front end was firmly lodged, and everyone stretched their legs on the soft golden sands, enjoying the ability to wander around freely after the constraints of the raft.

While the others lazed about on the beach, Glyn and Arki began the laborious climb up through the tumbled mass of blocks which they thought had once been a proud monument to man's progress, they little knew what the true purpose of the building or its contents had been.

They were about a third of the way up when they found a gap in the blocks large enough for them to walk into, taking them towards the core of the ruin.

'This part hasn't been damaged,' Arki pointed out, 'it's a solid square passageway, like those on the ship, except this is some kind of stone.'

'I'm going back to get the light thing, I don't think there will be enough natural light to go much further, and it could be dangerous,' said Glyn, 'you wait here, I'll not be long.' and he scuttled back through the tumble of blocks and out of sight. Being alone in a nearly dark pile of broken concrete wasn't Arki's idea of fun, and the more he thought about it, the more time dragged by.

At long last he could hear the scrambling footsteps of Glyn returning, puffing and panting as he came into the passage proper, his face red and perspiring with exertion.

'Bet you thought I'd stopped off for a meal and a rest.' gasped Glyn, trying to get his breath back.

'Damn right I did, it seemed like ages, I'm sure I heard some movement in here somewhere.'

'I doubt that very much. How could anything have got here, and if it had, how could it sustain itself, there's no vegetation on this island. Anyway, I was as quick as possible, perhaps your imagination got the better of you.' he added.

They managed to go a few more metres into the passage by letting their eyes get used to the gloom, but then they had to use the light projector.

Glyn found that by pressing the button on the end of the device the light would come on at full brilliance, and by accidentally twisting it, he found he could control the light level right down to a gentle glow.

'Didn't say anything about that in the instructions,' he said, 'perhaps if we run the light device as low as possible it will last that much longer, what do you think?'

'Makes sense to me.' Arki muttered, his eyes probing the darkness down the tunnel for anything which might pose a threat to them.

They had gone down the passage proper for about twenty metres when they came to a bend, and then the passage forked left and right, both sections looking identical.

Let's go down here,' Glyn indicated the passage to his right, 'if it leads nowhere, we can come back and try the other one.'

'Have you noticed there is much less in the way of sand and other rubbish in this section?' Arki asked, scuffing his feet to make the point.

'Yes, I would have expected more considering the time since this place last saw human feet, but maybe the curve in the tunnel and the jumble of rocks outside have something to do with it.' Glyn replied, feeling he ought to say something although it was of little interest to him.

As their eyes adapted to the low light, Glyn turned the button again, saving the power source a little more of its precious energy.

Another slight bend and their way was blocked by a massive door set in a frame, both made of the same shiny metal Arki had used to make his cutting blade from.

'There's a sort of wheel thing on the door, do you think we should turn it?' asked Glyn.

'Looks as if that's what it was intended for,' Arki replied, 'let's give it a try, I doubt we'll have much luck moving it after all this time though.'

Glyn put the light device on the floor of the passage, pointing it at the shiny door, and then they noticed some faded lettering just below the wheel.

'Can you read what it says?' asked Arki, straining his eyes in the dim light.

'No, it would seem to be in a language other than ours, I can't make any sense of it. Let's see if we can open this door.' Even with both of them gripping the wheel and putting all their weight behind the effort, it still refused to move.

'I know this might sound silly, but how about we try turning it the other way?' Arki raised his eyebrows to emphasize the question, which was totally lost on Glyn in the dim light of the lamp.

'OK.' he grunted, swinging his arms to loosen the muscles after straining them against the reluctant wheel.

The wheel turned a few millimetres, but they weren't sure if it had really moved or whether their hands had slipped.

'Come on, let's try again.' said Arki encouragingly, and strained until his eyes bulged from their sockets. When Glyn added his effort to the wheel, it moved, making a very high pitched screeching noise as bare metal rubbed on bare metal for the first time since the pulse missile had scored a direct hit on the complex so long ago.

When the wheel had been turned as far as it would go, there was a loud clunk, and when they pushed the door it groaned opened, just a little.

They both put their shoulders to the door and it creaked fully open, a cold draft of sterile air gushing into their faces, and taking them both by surprise.

'That air has a strange smell to it.' commented Glyn.

'A bit like the air in certain parts of the ship, when we found the service tunnel.' Arki added, briefly recalling the comparative comforts of their former life.

'Well, we've got it open, so we may as well see what's inside.' Glyn turned the little button on the lighting device, increasing the light output so that nothing would be missed which could pose a threat to their exploration.

The passage was featureless, just solid stone like walls, glass smooth and dust free, their footsteps echoing eerily.

After several twists and turns they came to another door, with the same type of wheel in its centre. This time it spun without much effort and the door opened easily.

Stepping through, they found themselves on a gallery which circled around a gigantic pit, in the middle of which stood a rocket of such enormous proportions that it made them gasp, and it was in pristine condition.

'Do you think this was the kind of thing they used to batter each other with?' asked an incredulous Arki, hardly able to believe his eyes.

'Certainly looks like it,' Glyn replied, 'small wonder there's so little of the world left intact if both sides had such huge weapons, and I have little doubt that they did.'

'According to what I read in the books, there were three main blocks of power, so if each of them were armed to the teeth with these, no one stood a chance of survival, so why start a conflict in the first place?' Arki was still trying to come to terms with the total insanity of the situation which must have prevailed at the time.

'They must have known what would happen once a war got started, and could foresee that it was inevitable, hence the project we were involved in.'

'So, as far as we know, all human life on earth was wiped out, and we are in effect the seeds preserved through time to repopulate what's left of the planet. Just about everything else must have been destroyed at the same time, I suppose.' Arki continued, desperately trying to see some reason in a totally unreasonable scenario.

Glyn remained silent, turning the light device up to full brilliance and gazing at the massive weapon of destruction poised in its silo, still looking ready to deliver its deadly payload of oblivion to some unsuspecting section of the earth's crust.

'Don't worry Arki, I can't make any sense of it either,' he said at long last, 'some life forms must have survived, and probably mutated in the overwhelming wash of radiation which must have been present at the time, or we wouldn't have anything growing here at all. What a terrible waste though.'

They stood there for some time, just looking at the beautifully streamlined shape of the missile which concealed such a hideous cargo within its gleaming shell.

'Well, we at least know what this place was all about, and it looks as if someone else did also, and got their poke in first. Want to go down that stairway and see what's at the bottom?' Glyn asked, keen to see how such a terrible weapon was controlled.

It took quite a time for them to descend to the lower level of the silo, and in the last few metres they had to enter another doorway with its ubiquitous wheel.

The passageway wound downwards, eventually coming out into what they supposed was the control room, a vast array of blank screens and key pads sat on desks protruding from the walls.

'It seems hideously strange that people sat here and decided which section of the opposing force's country they would obliterate, and then pressed a button and sat back to watch a section of earth seared out of existence. How could things have got into such a terrible state?' Arki asked.

'The history of Earth I read in the books didn't go right up to the point where it all went wrong, but I could read between the lines and see the trends forming which would lead to outright total war, if no one put the brakes on, and it seemed no one did.'

They wandered around the missile control room, marvelling at the equipment and trying to figure out how it worked, but were afraid to actually touch anything, in case it did.

The journey back up to the outside was long and arduous, and it was a very tired pair who eventually joined the others in the warm sunlight on the beach to recount their find, and try to explain how it figured in the general scheme of things.

After telling their tale, it seemed as if the sun had lost some of its warmth and the sands weren't so soft and golden. Glyn called for the evening meal to be brought forward to cheer everyone up a little.

Early next morning they were on there way again, after a bit of a struggle getting the raft afloat. Glyn gave orders to try and get the raft over to the right-hand side of the river bank once they had got underway, so that fresh water could be found and the supplies of food replenished, but this proved to be a little more difficult than giving the orders.

The current caused the raft to twist and turn as the uneven river bed guided the water hither and thither, and those using the poles found that one moment they could get a good purchase and push the raft on course, and then there was deep water beneath them and the poles were useless.

This caused one unfortunate to fall overboard as his pole found nothing solid beneath it, and he toppled over the side amid much laughter. He was only saved by the quick reaction of Arki who threw him a length of creeper.

Once they had got clear of the strange island and its under watercurrents, the river returned to its old self and the raft drifted along in a more soberly fashion, being gradually guided by those with the poles across towards the bank, although they occasionally found an extra deep channel and had to let it drift where it chose.

The shallow water nearer the bank gave them much more control over the raft, and it was now just a matter of finding a suitable cove or inlet in which to beach the craft.

After an hour or so, the only inlet which looked at all promising had a solid wall of forest coming right down to the water's edge and was inaccessible for landing.

'Let's try poling up the tributary a bit.' Glyn called out encouragingly, and got a series of dirty looks from those with the job of poling the craft against the current.

Slowly the raft lumbered up the stream and around several bends, and there before them was a perfect landing place.

A gently sloping bank of sand swept down from a grassy lawn behind which could be seen clusters of the black berry bearing bushes.

'Right, let's go for that.' called Glyn, swinging his arm out to indicate the beach.

The raft had doubled its speed by the time it reached the shore, and then ground to a halt catapulting several of its passengers prematurely onto the soft sand amid shrieks of laughter from those who saw what was about to happen and had braced themselves for the impact, remembering what had happened the last time.

The water in the tributary was fit to drink, and everyone had their fill before breaking up into little groups to gather food from the nearby forest, and firewood to keep the chill night air at bay.

As the sun dipped below the horizon, the fire was blazing merrily, everyone had eaten as much of the bounteous gifts of the forest as was deemed sensible, and the emergency rations had been spared once more, much to Glyn's relief.

As darkness crowded in around them like a silent black cloak, the fire was stoked up, sending twisting clouds of sparks spiralling up into the cold night air and casting dense elongated shadows of the sitters around the fire on the surrounding sands, like the spokes of a wheel.

Stories were told to entertain the younger ones, Mia got Glyn to feel the kicking bulge of the baby growing inside her, insisting it was trying to get out despite what he said, and everyone agreed it had been a very good day, except Brendon who had eaten too much fruit and spent most of the evening trotting back and forth to the bushes amid ribald comments from just about everyone.

They were just getting ready to sleep when a piercing scream rent the otherwise still night air, and all motion froze for a moment as no one was quite sure where the wail of death had come from.

'That's much too close for comfort,' Glyn said quietly, his eyes straining into the impenetrable darkness of the night, 'we'd better spend the night on the raft, mooring it a few metres out in the stream.'

'How about some soft bedding to sleep on, those logs are damned hard.' someone suggested.

'It's too dark to risk fumbling about looking for ferns,' Arki replied, muttering to himself, 'I don't believe this.'

'How about your lighting device?' the same voice rejoined.

'We're not wasting that on a few ferns, you're amply covered to withstand a night on the logs, just think about those who aren't.' Arki spat back, having identified the voice as the one who had recently returned from the bushes.

The firewood stock was quickly carried to the water's edge, flaming brands from the old fire soon created a new one on a spit of sand which jutted out a little way into the river, and the raft was eased off the beach, the two mooring creepers being attached to staves driven into the sandbank.

'OK, everyone onto the raft, Glyn softly called out, 'I want two guards with sharpened staves, one facing the water and one facing the bank. Keep a sharp lookout, if anything moves, I want to know about it. As soon as you feel drowsy, wake someone else up to take your place, we can't afford to make any mistakes. Oh, and someone should go ashore to stoke the fire up whenever it needs it, we need to be able to see if anything fancies us.'

With the raft moored several metres off shore, they felt a little safer, but it was difficult to get to sleep, and not just because of the hard logs.

What little sleep they did achieve was rudely broken twice during the long night, as something became a meal for something further up the food chain, and Glyn decided that food gatherers in the future would have to be accompanied by guards armed with pointed poles as there was no way of judging the physical size of the new threat to their existence.

Dawn broke none too soon for the sleep starved travellers, and all were a bit grumpy as they ate the remains of the fruit and nuts from the previous night. After the terrifying sounds emitted from the forest during the hours of darkness none were too keen to get more, despite their hunger.

'Top up your water supplies and let's get the food replenished. Remember, no one goes into the forest without armed guards in future until we know just what's in there.' Glyn was just as keen to move on as everyone else, the anguished shrieks of last night still echoed in his mind.

The foraging party returned from the trees with indecent haste and clambered on board the raft, the mooring ties were released, and the craft began its slow drift back to the main river, helped along by those with the guiding poles.

'I've had a look at the lashings which hold the logs together to see if any have loosened,' said Arki, 'and they all seem secure. What is surprising is that some have sprouted new growth, and given time could be used to reinforce the existing bindings.' Glyn went to have a look, and was surprised at the speed with which the new shoots had developed in so short a time.

'The creepers must be getting nutrient as well as water from the river, pity the tree trunks weren't alive as well, the raft might grow to become a ship!' Glyn then had to explain what a ship was to one of the onlookers, but gave up after a while as no light of comprehension had dawned on him.

They joined the main river and the raft picked up speed again, but it wasn't until small waves began to appear that Glyn became worried.

'Looks like the river is getting a bit narrower.' he said to Arki, who was standing at the front end looking out for submerged obstacles.

'I think you're right, it would certainly account for the increase in velocity.' Arki liked technical terms.

Soon it became apparent that they were heading for a narrow gorge as the sides of the river closed in, and great cliffs towered above them as the raft picked up speed.

By now the guiding poles were useless as the river had deepened, and they were no longer able to reach the bottom.

'If we hit the side we're finished,' Glyn called out, a touch of panic in his voice, 'the raft will be ripped to shreds, and us along with it. If we get too close, push against the rocks, but be careful you don't get the pole jammed in a crevice and lose your balance.'

The waves had grown in magnitude as the gorge narrowed still further, and were now causing the raft to ripple like a shaken rug as the timbers ran from side to side, and the lashing allowed a small amount of movement between them.

'Two men with poles on each side,' Arki shouted against the roar of the turbulent waters, taking one of the poles himself, 'the rest lie down and hold onto the lashings. Those nearest the 'polers', hold onto their feet in case they lose their balance and get swept overboard.'

Now the raft bucked and kicked like a frightened mule as waves caused by the water hitting the sides of the gorge rebounded back across, and the shelter they had so carefully built in the middle of the raft swayed dangerously.

Glyn quickly checked to see if their backpacks were safely lashed down. Fortunately, someone had sensibly arranged the backpacks in the form of an enclosure, the fruit and other edibles being held in the centre.

The waters had now taken on a dirty grey colour due to the restricted amount of light reaching into the gorge, and ahead there loomed another obstacle to their progress south.

What looked like a solid wall of rock closed off the ever narrowing gorge, and as they bobbed and bounced along, they found themselves in the bottom of a narrow trough, the water on either side of them rising up well above their heads where it touched the walls of the gorge in a foaming line.

'Why has the water risen up each side of us like that?' asked Glyn of Arki, holding on to one of his legs with one hand and the lashing of the raft with the other.

'Must be due to the shape of the river bed and the acceleration of the water in this narrowing section of the gorge, I would think,' Arki shouted back against the roar of the waters, 'must say it looks frightening whatever the reason might be.' he concluded.

The raft sped along the bottom of the depression in the racing waters, thankfully the upsweep of the water on each side of it keeping it centred in the trough.

'Where the hell's all this water going?' asked Glyn, his view lessened because of his lying down on the raft.

'Can't see very well, it would seem to go up to the end wall of the gorge and disappear somewhere. Maybe there's a big hole in the river bed!'

Glyn's string of expletives at Arki's light-hearted comment were entirely lost to all in the overpowering roar of a lot of water trying to get into a space far too small for it.

The light seemed to fade even more as the towering cliffs on each side closed in overhead, and the raft raced on towards the approaching end wall of solid rock.

The white line of seething foam where the raised water met the edge of the cliffs had disappeared, and as the river widened slightly, the water returned to its more normal level on each side of the speeding raft.

They suddenly noticed the tumultuous roar of the convulsing river was gone, the waters were now black and perfectly smooth as they raced towards the rapidly advancing end of the gorge in an eerie silence.

'This is it, whatever it is,' Arki yelled out, 'hold on tight.' And the raft tipped over at a horribly precarious angle.

The light level was so low, it was almost like twilight as the raft and its occupants slid down the glassy smooth slope of dark water into the yawning maw of the cavern in the rock face.

Arki and the other three with the guiding poles instinctively dropped down to hold on to the lashings, not knowing how much head room there would be as the raft rushed headlong into the darkness.

Glyn wished he had retrieved his light device from the pack before they had entered the cavern. But it was too late now, in the darkness which surrounded them he was unable to tell which was his pack amongst the others.

'Hold on tight everyone.' he called out in what was almost total silence except for the faintest chuckling of the water between the logs.

The angle of the raft suddenly changed again, returning to its former level position in the water, and with it came the first natural sound they had heard since entering the darkness of the tunnel.

It was a deep almost subsonic sound, felt rather than heard, and imaginations ran riot trying to make out what could be causing it. The very air seemed to shimmer with the sound as it swept up the tunnel, and then it was gone, the eerie silence returning once more.

There was a sharp crack as the top of the shelter hit a low portion of the tunnel roof, breaking all four uprights in one blow and causing several yells of protest from those who were hit by the poles and the roof covering as it collapsed.

'Hold onto the bits if you can,' Arki called out, 'we may need them later.'

A faint glimmer of light up ahead broke the inky blackness through which they had been travelling, and Glyn announced,

'I think we're through, but keep your heads down for a while, there might be some projections in the roof.'

Slowly the light grew in intensity until they could clearly see the smooth roof of the tunnel, burnished over time by the fine grains of sand which the river had picked up when in full flood and had filled the tunnel completely.

The raft seemed to be slowing up as the light increased, and Arki rose to his feet now there was plenty of head room.

Picking up his pole, he tried to find how deep the water was, but the pole didn't reach the river bed even when he lay down to gain that extra bit of depth.

Glyn, looking directly ahead, suddenly shouted a warning,

'Get over to the side of the tunnel, use your poles on the roof and make it quick.'

The tunnel opened out to nearly three times its normal width and consequently the river had slowed down considerably, to disappear into space as it left the cavern.

'Come on, use those poles,' yelled Glyn, grabbing a pole himself, 'if we don't make it to the side and hold on, we'll be over the edge.'

The raft bumped along the side of the tunnel walls, but despite many eager hands, no one was able to get a grip on the smooth rock.

Just as they thought they were going to be catapulted into the air as the river surged over the lip of the giant water fall, the raft caught on a small outcrop of rock on the very edge of the lip itself, and shuddered to a halt.

'Nobody move until we see how stable the situation is.' Arki called out, and everyone froze, realizing that one false move could dislodge the raft and send it over the edge.

He carefully worked his way up to the leading edge of the craft and looked down into the dark water below.

'Although the piece of rock I can see just below the surface of the water is small, it extends on each side for quite a way, and I think the raft is quite safely lodged against it. I'll take a look over the edge of the falls to see if we can get down in one piece.'

Arki wriggled forward as far as he could to peer over the curve of dark water, two of the others holding onto his ankles to make sure he didn't slip over the edge. After a few moments he squirmed his way back from the edge, ashen faced and looking none too happy.

'Well, what can you see?' asked Glyn, fearing the worst.

'The river doesn't just fall away in a cascade, but goes down a long slope as it did when we entered the tunnel. It is quite smooth in its flow, but goes down a very long way to level out in a seemingly normal flow of water.'

'Good, that means we can probably go down it as before, so why the long face?' asked Glyn.

'Well, it starts off like a normal river, and then goes into a huge circular basin with a giant whirlpool in the middle. There's no way we can get past it that I can see, even if we get down the slope in one piece to start with.'

'If there isn't any debris in the middle, then it means if we get caught up in the spinning water, we should eventually get spun out again.' Glyn reasoned.

'There isn't any debris in the middle because there isn't a middle, what I mean is that the water spins around and then disappears down the hole in the middle, and we would follow if we got caught up in the spin.' Arki was having difficulty finding the words to describe what he had seen.

Just then a low frequency vibration seemed to make everything shudder as the whirlpool took a hand in deciding what they could or couldn't do.

The water in the middle suddenly stopped falling into the hole, and welled back up to form a huge bulge which hovered for a few moments before accelerating upwards in a glistening white column.

Countless millions of litres of water screamed out of the centre of the whirlpool to shoot up into the clear blue sky, soon followed by a colossal burst of boiling white water vapour which formed a huge seething cloud around the base of the ascending column.

Slowly, as in a dream, the huge water column collapsed back into the basin with a thunderous roar, sending a wave of boiling white foam high up the sides of the basin and creating a brilliant double rainbow, then, as the foaming waters subsided, the whirlpool slowly began its twisting dance around the depression in the river bed once again.

Glyn had by now crawled up to the front edge of the raft, and standing up saw for himself the devastating effect the whirlpool and its descending column of water would have had on their somewhat fragile craft if it had been swept over the edge of the lip they were now caught on.

'We're stuck here by the looks of it. There's no other way out of this tunnel, and we can't even crawl down the sides of the water slide because they're too smooth.' Glyn said.

Arki crawled up to the front end of the raft once more and stayed until another cycle of the whirlpool had taken place.

'You know, I think we might just make it if we time it right. As you say, there's no other way down, so we either stay here and starve or take a chance on the raft. What we need is something to throw into the water and time its progress to the whirlpool. It'll need to be something big or we shan't be able to see it clearly when it reaches the area of the basin.'

Nine:
The Art of Surviving

'IF WE GET it just right, we should arrive at the edge of the basin just before the bulge comes up, and then slip past it before the whole thing shoots up into the air. We may get a little wet, but it's better than just staying here.'

'What can we use to throw over.' Glyn asked, and they both looked at Brendon who shrank back with a look of horror on his face.

'Don't be so silly, we're only joking, you wouldn't be big enough.' Arki felt sorry for the man.

'Oh, I don't know, we could get him to wave his tunic just before the whirlpool sucked him into the middle, we should be able to see that from here.' Glyn couldn't help having one more go at the gullible unfortunate.

'How about the remains of the side screen, that's quite big and should float well.' someone suggested.

'Good idea.' said Glyn, a little hope returning to his voice.

The screen was disentangled from the rest of the wreckage brought about by the shelter hitting the roof of the tunnel, and Glyn stood by with an eye to his timekeeper as the side shield was thrown overboard when the whirlpool went into its spinning action after the collapse of the water column.

They timed its journey down the water slope and along the river to the point where it was pulled into the vortex of the whirlpool, and it then disappeared from sight. A short while later the whirlpool erupted in its customary fashion, but there was no sight of the shield amid the general uproar of the water column as it cleaved the heavens and then crashed back down to the basin.

'Getting the timing right is going to be crucial if we are to come out of this in one piece.' Glyn said with little confidence in his voice.

'I've noticed one thing which may help,' Arki interjected, 'and that's when the bulge of water comes up from the hole, it sets up a big wave which bounces around the basin, but on the far side the wave seems to carry on down the river. If we could get the raft into position so that the wave picks it up, we would be quickly swept away from the collapsing water column and on down the river.'

'I don't know if we can time it that accurately, but it's certainly worth a try.' Glyn said, and then proceeded to tell the others what he proposed to do.

The remains of the shelter was securely lashed down over the backpacks and the remaining food stocks, and everyone was drilled in what they had to do when the raft was released from the rock holding it at the lip of the water slide.

'Everyone spread out over the raft, and check the lashings around your area are holding securely. Make a loop with any of the new growths or lose ends of the creepers to put your feet in, and make sure you have a good hand hold. If anyone goes overboard, don't try to save them, you could get swept away as well. If anyone does get thrown off, try to keep afloat and as near the raft as possible, and we'll pick you up once we're past the basin. Good luck everyone, and hold on.'

Glyn went through the timing sequence once more, and then he and Arki used the poles to lever the raft free of the rock which had held them safely at the lip of the water slide, and they were off.

The raft gave a sickening lurch as it went over the lip of the slide, and seemed to drop like a stone as it picked up speed on the silently flowing water chute. There were several screams as the raft accelerated downwards, despite the fact that the motion of the raft was as smooth as silk.

As the raft reached the bottom of the water slide and the horizon tilted back to its more normal position, Glyn raised his head a little to see how near the whirlpool they were.

'I think we're being swept out to one side of the main swirl.' he said, as an eerie hissing noise filled the air.

As they raced towards the seething maelstrom of the whirlpool, the raft tilted up on one side, and they were trapped in the swirling waters as they spun ever inwards to disappear down the hole in the centre.

The angle of tilt grew even steeper as the raft was drawn inwards, and all they could see was the opposite side of the dark funnel of water as it spun faster and faster towards the dark abyss of the massive geyser.

Those brave enough to raise their heads to confront what seemed to be the inevitable end to their journey in the new world, were too paralysed with fear to scream, and so the raft spun on downwards to the accompaniment of the ear splitting hiss of the falling waters.

Just when all seemed lost, the raft returned to its level position and then tilted in the opposite direction. The hole was filled, and the bulge had begun.

As the enormous column of water began its journey up from the depths of the hole, the raft tilted even more steeply, and once again they could see the surrounding basin and the river trailing off into the distance.

The bulge in the middle of the whirlpool grew higher, and the raft was lifted up on the wave caused by the change of direction of the water flow.

They had come down the main water slide at a fair speed, but it was nothing compared to the velocity the raft now had as the wave raced away from the huge column of water which was tearing skywards behind them.

The deep gorge they were in narrowed a little, and the wave with the raft atop its crest, sped up as the water tried to find more room for itself in an ever decreasing channel.

Arki let out a yell of triumph as he released the tension which had built up over the last few minutes, and a ragged chorus of cheers rang out from those who had managed to draw enough breath into their lungs to do so.

The sky seemed to darken as the massive water column went ever higher, and then it collapsed. They felt the shock wave before the water hit them in a series of stunning blows which threatened to smash the raft and its travellers into pulp.

The thunderous noise of the water returning to the basin reverberated along the gorge, hurting their ears, but none were willing to chance letting go of their grip on the raft's lashing to protect their tortured eardrums.

After what seemed an age, the falling mass of water receded to heavy rain, and the wave which had sped them to safety lost momentum as the gorge widened. Glyn stood up carefully to see where they were in relation to the whirlpool. It was now safely some distance behind them, and as he encouraged the others to regain their feet, the rain turned to drizzle and then stopped altogether.

The warmth of the sun was very welcome after the drenching and pummelling they had received, and it wasn't long before a more cheerful mood had manifested itself, the odd joke being greeted with copious amounts of nervous laughter, thus releasing the tremendous tension they had all been under. 'I must admit, I did have my doubts as to whether we would make it through that maelstrom of a whirlpool, but we did, so perhaps we can reach the southern areas we were instructed to find after all.'

Glyn was feeling pleased and relieved that they had all survived against seemingly impossible odds yet again, and his old confidence returned.

The raft was back in its drifting mode now, gently guided by two men with poles to keep it not too far from the bank.

A little high cloud had obscured the sun, making it difficult for Glyn to judge what direction they were actually going in, although he assumed that the river was still heading south as they hadn't encountered any bends in the water flow worth mentioning.

'I think we should find somewhere to land soon. It would be good to stretch our legs on something solid again after what we've been through, and we'll need to find a place for tonight anyway.' Glyn was planning ahead again as he assumed responsibility for all those under his care.

The raft drifted on, several streams joining the main flow, but none offering the kind of beach they were looking for. A short way ahead, a rocky outcrop jutted out into the river and the guide poles were used to push the raft out into the main stream to avoid grounding the craft on the rocks.

What they hadn't seen was the fast moving river exiting into the main flow just behind the rocky promontory, and the raft was whisked out into the middle of the river before they knew what had happened.

'I can't reach the bottom,' one of the 'polers' called out, 'so I can't steer the raft. What shall we do?' There was little they could do, except hope that the current would eventually return them to the bank on one side of the river or the other.

Most of the raft's occupants were either lying down or sitting with their legs dangling in the warm water, relaxing, when Arki called out with a touch of raw panic in his voice,

'Look over there, what do you think is causing that?'

About five hundred metres up stream, and heading straight for them, something very big was moving along just below the surface. The bow wave was nearly a metre high, the water humped up and then falling away from the submarine shape, without a sign of foam or other disturbance to the river's normally smooth surface.

'Oh no, I thought things were going too smoothly.' Glyn muttered to himself as he heaved his tired body to its feet.

Whatever it was, had slowed down to almost match the speed of the raft, which was about the same as the river flow. Glyn had now joined Arki at the rear of the craft, and together they armed themselves with poles just in case they could use them to some advantage.

With slow deliberation, the gargantuan grey shape changed course slightly to drift by underneath them, with barely a millimetre to spare.

The raft was quickly lifted up a few centimetres by the surge of water beneath it, although the creature was only travelling a little faster than the raft itself. One of the onlookers standing at the very edge of the craft and paralysed with fear at what he had seen, fell overboard as the huge shape glided beneath them.

Unable to swim, he lay thrashing about in the water and yelling his head off every time he came up for a gasp of air.

'Calm down,' Glyn called out, 'stop waving your arms about and you'll float, just lie back in the water and we'll get you out.' He didn't know how though, as the man had drifted some distance away by now, and was well out of reach of their longest pole.

The man did as he was bid, only to start yelling again when he realized that help wasn't forthcoming from the raft as the distance between them slowly increased.

Still the giant shape silently glided by beneath them, with hardly a ripple showing on either side of the raft, and it was only when the tail section passed by that they had some idea of the creature's overall size.

Arki and Glyn stood looking at each other, dumbfounded.

'I don't believe this, nothing can grow that big.' Arki said, shaking his head in disbelief.

'Well it moves, it lined itself up with the raft and was careful not to overturn us, so we must assume it has life and some form of intelligence.' Glyn said, but without much conviction in his voice.

After they had recovered their composure a little, Arki said, 'What shall we do for our friend in the water, he's drifting further away by the minute.'

'Damned if I know,' Glyn replied, frustrated at not being able to offer help. Just then Arki looked ahead of the raft, and saw the huge underwater creature turn in a great circle, heading for the man in the water, who was now some hundred metres away.

'Do you think it's going to eat him?' asked Glyn, who had now seen the creature as well.

'Why else would it turn back from its course?' replied Arki, horrified at what he had just said.

The marine creature manoeuvred itself around until it was in a direct line with the man in the water and the raft, and then it slowly cruised forward towards the living bait which was now in paralytic shock at its impending demise, and lay still in the water.

The metre high ripple on the surface of the river denoting the presence of the submarine creature slowly crept up on its target, and then passed him, the ripple dying away as the colossal shape beneath came to a sudden halt.

The watchers on the raft fully expected to see a cavernous mouth open and swallow the unfortunate man in one piece, but it didn't. A huge ripple sped away from the pair as the creature changed position, and then a massive smooth dark grey head eased itself out of the water with the luckless man perched on top. Two small but brilliant dark blue eyes looked down on the raft and its occupants, slowly scanning the vessel from end to end.

A slight turbulence in the water behind the creature indicated that it was on the move, and slowly the distance between it and the raft decreased until it was towering above them, completely dwarfing the tiny craft.

The vast creature somehow changed the shape of its head, or maybe it was the creature's version of a frown, and the man who was perched up on top slid down the slight depression on the front of its head with arms and legs flailing, and landed in the water at the edge of the raft.

Eager hands grabbed the spluttering man and pulled him onboard, they turned to see what would happen next.

Again the turbulence at the rear of the creature, and it slowly slid backwards from them, as if it knew that was the only thing it could do without tipping them all into the water.

Having achieved what it considered to be a safe distance from the raft, the huge creature turned and headed down river at high speed, a two metre high bow wave being the only sign of its existence.

'I can't get over the size of it,' Arki exclaimed, 'how can such a creature exist? And those eyes! They had the look of intelligence in them, and I found that quite unnerving.'

'Just as well the creature was friendly, it could surely have made a real mess of our raft, and had us as a snack into the bargain.' Glyn added, breathing a sigh of relief.

'What worries me,' said Arki, 'is that for a creature that big, there must be an awful lot of others which it eats, and they could well be big enough to eat us, not that I want to spread alarm and despondency.'

'So far, we haven't seen anything else, so perhaps it eats plants.' Glyn said hopefully, and the matter was dropped for the time being.

The raft gently glided on down the river which was getting very wide again, and a concerted effort with the poles was made to try and guide it back towards the bank with little effect, as the poles didn't have enough purchase on the water to make much difference to the direction of drift.

Brendon finally came to the rescue with an idea which astounded them all, Glyn and Arki in retrospect feeling a bit miffed and surprised that they hadn't thought of it first.

'Why don't we take off our jackets and hold them up for the wind to blow into them, its going in the general direction of the bank and that should pull us along.' he said with a smile at Glyn.

'You know, you really astound me sometimes,' said Glyn, 'I think we ought to consider making you the leader.'

'Oh no, I'm not clever enough for that, besides, if I got it wrong, I'd never hear the end of it.' He was probably right on that point.

Glyn got all the men together and explained the basic idea.

'If we all take our jackets off and stand in a row holding the jackets stretched out between us, they will catch the wind and hopefully drive us towards the river bank, in fact, if we tie two jackets together one above the other, using the arms, it would be even more effective,' turning towards Brendon and reluctantly adding, 'it was his idea.' patting him on the shoulder. Brendon generously beamed at all and sundry.

With pairs of jackets joined by the arms, and the men strung out along the length of the raft, the gentle wind filled the home-made sails. It was difficult to tell at first if they were making any progress until one bright spark stuck two poles up some distance apart, and by lining them up with his eye was able to tell that the raft was indeed being driven towards the river bank, albeit very slowly.

Once it was apparent that the system was working, volunteers came forward to relieve the aching arms of the jacket holders, the women joining in until everyone had had a spell at being a ship's mast.

'The pole is reaching the bottom.' someone called out, and the sails were returned to their rightful owners, while the 'polers' got to work to bring the raft closer inshore.

The river bank had changed in character after passing the promontory where the tributary had swept them into midstream, and was now composed of rocks in the few places where the forest didn't come down to the water's edge.

They landed late in the evening, having at last found a stretch of sand to beach the raft on, and then had to eat some of the emergency rations as it was too dark to risk going into the forest to gather fruit.

Next day the food gatherers were doubly keen to replenish their fruit stocks, as they were now more used to a natural diet and much preferred it to the food concentrates brought from the ship so long ago.

Four guards armed with pointed poles accompanied them just to be on the safe side, although they had seen no animals in the forests so far, and later stocks of two new fruits and a different nut were added to their larder.

Later, one of the women came up to Glyn and quietly said,

'I think Mia is nearly ready to give birth to your child.'

'I don't see how that can be,' replied Glyn, looking surprised, 'there hasn't been enough time for the child to fully form yet. Are you sure she isn't just making a fuss about it to get my attention? I haven't been very attentive of late I must admit, what with all the problems we've had.'

'No, I don't think so. I've had a child, and I know all the symptoms. I think you should make arrangements for the birth fairly soon, you don't want it to happen on the raft in the middle of the river when we're being chased by something.' The woman turned away, she had said her piece and it was now up to him.

Glyn conferred with Arki about the matter, but he didn't know any more about it than Glyn did.

They spent the rest of the day at the landing place, building up their food stocks and tightening the bindings on the raft ready for the next stage of their journey.

The big hacking blade made by Arki proved very useful when one of the food parties went a little deeper into the forest to find new food. The undergrowth in some areas seemed to have exploded in growth, and the hacking blade made it possible for them to penetrate far deeper into the forest than ever before.

That evening, Mia was visibly in distress with the huge bulge that was once a flat taut stomach, and Glyn felt sorry for his lack of attention and help in her uncomfortable state, not that there was a lot he could have done about it.

The contractions began a short while after their meal, and before Glyn could work himself up into a total state of panic, he was pushed to one side by two of the women, and told to go and do something useful in no uncertain terms.

They led Mia away to join the rest of the women, who knew what was about to happen.

He had never been spoken to like that before, and the firmness with which they had ordered him away made him realize that leadership was a thing of ephemeral consent, and could easily be blown away by the lightest of winds when the occasion arose.

Glyn and Arki went down to the water's edge to join a couple of the other men as there was nothing useful they could do, or would be allowed to do. Glyn was satisfied that Mia was in good hands with the other women.

They had been sitting there for a while, just chatting in the half light of evening, when Arki noticed one of the men furthest from him was quietly fiddling away with something. 'What are you doing?' he asked, having moved along the beach a little to get a better view of what the man was making. 'I'm going to try and find out if there is any life in these waters. I've attached a fine strand of creeper to this stick, and if I can find something alive to put on the end, I'll dangle it out over the river. If there's anything hungry out there, it might be tempted to take a bite.'

'Where did you get that idea from?' asked Arki, surprised by the man's ingenuity. 'I worked it out for myself, it seems quite reasonable to me.' Arki was impressed at the man's reasoning ability, and resolved to include him in solving any future problems they might have as they as they made their way south.

'And just what do you propose to attach to your line Greg?'

'A wriggling grub like creature. I found one in a rotten log I trod on in the forest, so there should be more.' Greg replied.

Greg left his stick and the attached creeper line at the water's edge, and without saying a word to anyone, went up the sand bank towards the glow of the camp fire, and disappeared from view.

'You know,' Arki said quietly to Glyn, 'that's one bright fellow. I wouldn't have thought of making a trapping line like that, perhaps we should include him in any future decision making.'

'Seems a good idea, lets see if he catches anything first.' They both lay back on the soft sand, looking up at the first of the evening stars which had begun to dust the velvet deep blue of the sky.

A rustle of hurried footsteps awoke them from their reverie.

'Did you manage to find anything suitable?' asked Arki, interested in the outcome of the fishing experiment.

'Yes, I found this.' Greg held out a white wriggling maggot, which by its gyrations had somehow sensed its forthcoming fate. He wound several turns of the fine creeper strand around the middle of the unfortunate creature, picked up the stick and walked over to a large rock which jutted out into the river.

Glyn and Arki followed, climbing up after the fisherman and positioning themselves either side of him as he sat down to dangle his line in the now black waters of the river.

All three sat there for about half an hour, enjoying the serenity of the scene and the cool breeze which swept in from the river, when Greg's home-made line gave a twitch.

'Something's interested in the bait.' he said, and gently pulled the line in towards the rock they were sitting on.

The line suddenly went taut, and then twanged as something on the other end sensed it had been trapped. Greg nearly fell into the water as he was about to lean over to get a better view of what he had caught. Arki grabbed his jacket and held him steady as he reached down to get hold of the creeper, and giving it a wrench, swung his catch over his shoulder and onto the back end of the rock.

All three scrambled to their feet and hurried over to where the creature had landed, slowing down as they approached it. A soggy thumping sound came from a long dark body, almost a metre and a half long and as thick as a mans arm, it lay thrashing about in fury on the dark rock, so they were unable to see the finer details of what they had caught.

'Let's get it into the light,' said Arki, 'it may be equipped with teeth.' The creature seemed to be firmly attached to the line, so they dragged it up the sand bank and into the light of the camp fire, which was now burning brightly.

When the others around the fire saw what the hunters had brought in they all backed away in a hurry, but curiosity got the better of them, and slowly they drew a little closer as the creature, unused to so much heat and light, lay still.

The creeper line had got tangled around several of the vicious ten centimetre long curved teeth which protruded from both jaws, and a slow trickle of water dribbled out between them to stain the sand with a dark patch around its now still head. Glyn edged a little closer, and gave it a poke.

'I think it's dead, at least I hope it is.' he said, giving it another push with his foot. The creature didn't move, but Glyn wasn't taking any chances. Picking up a piece of wood from the edge of the fire, he gave it a smart blow just behind the shiny grey green head, but the only movement they could discern was from the blow. The eyes, as black and evil as they looked, were as dead as the rest of the creature.

'Do you think we could eat it?' someone from the back of the crowd asked, 'if we make it hot first, I don't fancy it raw.'

'We can but try,' Glyn replied, 'we'll cook it over the fire to make sure it is sterilized, and if the food test is passed, you can be the first to try some.'

There was no reply from the back of the crowd.

Arki removed the head, as this was the most off putting part of the creature, and then split it from end to end, emptying out the internal organs. Winding it around a thick stick proved a little more difficult than they had imagined, but it was achieved in the end, and then it was mounted just above the flames to cook.

Glyn suddenly remembered Mia, and enquired as to her whereabouts, to be informed that she was with several of the other women and had given birth to a boy. He felt ashamed not to have paid her more attention considering what was about to happen, and now it had happened, and he hadn't been on hand to help.

And then he remembered the off hand way he had been dismissed earlier by the other two women, but he still felt bad about it.

As he approached the little knot of women on the other side of the camp fire, Mia looked up at him and smiled sweetly. 'Look what we have got,' she said proudly, holding up the infant in her outstretched arms, 'aren't I clever?'

'You certainly are.' was all he could think of to say, and sat down beside her in the space one of the other women had made for him.

After a few minutes of general chat to Mia and the other women, he found himself holding the new infant somewhat awkwardly in his arms, but when it began to cry Mia took it back gently and put it to her breast, and all was peace and quiet around the camp fire once again.

'Glyn, will you come and have a look at this?' someone from the other side of the fire called out, and relieved, he excused himself from the company of the ladies to attend to matters more befitting to his gender.

'I think the thing is cooked,' said Arki, 'at least the flesh is soft when I poke it with a stick. Shall we try it?'

'We've gone this far, so why not? I'll break a little bit off and we'll do the under the tongue test.'

It took two of them to lift the eel down from its cooking position, and the mouth-watering smell brought the others a little closer.

'OK, where's our friend who wanted to eat the creature?' asked Arki, and after a bit of pushing and shoving, a rather reluctant member of the group stood before them.

'Don't look so worried, I'm the official tester,' Arki said with a laugh, 'but if it's safe, you can have the first full portion, OK?' By the look on the man's face, he didn't seem too sure if it was.

Arki did the test, and after the prescribed time, ate a small portion and sat down by the fire to join the others as they went over the day's events.

Half an hour later, with Arki suffering no ill effects, the eel was considered fit to eat and the reluctant proposer of the idea was winkled out of the crowd once more and offered the first helping.

With all the others looking on, he had little option other than to put a brave face on it and take a bite. After a few chews on the new food, the look on his face had the others queuing up for their ration, and before long there was little left except the bones.

A helping of fruit and nuts finished off the evening meal, and everyone sat back to relax after a long hard day's work and talk about the gargantuan water monster which had surprised them all.

Just before the night watch was posted and the others took a well earned sleep, Arki quietly took Glyn to one side.

'Have you noticed that all the woman are pregnant? Some have bigger bumps in front than others, but I'm told they're all with child,' Arki said, 'can't think why I didn't spot it before though.'

'Well, I didn't spot it,' said Glyn, 'but there has been a lot happening lately. Looking back on things, I think when we were on the ship there must have been something in the food or water which prevented pregnancies, and that's how births were controlled. Now that element is missing, and so there is no control, but what I don't understand is the speed with which Mia's child developed and was born. It seemed to take longer on the ship, so how do you explain that?'

'Can't really, but then there's a lot of things I can't explain.' Arki was now getting into his stride and looking at things which had been at the back of his mind for some time.

'Did you notice that the doorway in the concrete building where we sheltered from the storm was made for people nearly twice our height? And the control panels in that strange building on the island, they were far too high for us to operate easily without sitting on very high stools.' Arki paused for breath, Glyn didn't say anything, so he continued.

'I can't quite put my finger on it, but things here seem to be a bit bigger than I would have expected somehow, and looking back on it, the ship seemed to be a bit more spacious than it needed to be. Do you think we've been genetically shrunk for some reason, to conserve supplies when on the ship?'

'I wouldn't think so, the ship was designed to cater for our needs, so there would be little point is making us smaller. But maybe something else has had that effect. Now that you mention these anomalies, I can see them too, but I can't explain them.'

'I don't think we should mention these things to the others at this stage.' Arki said, and Glyn agreed. They went their separate ways for the night, Glyn seeking out Mia and offering a few words of comfort after her birthing ordeal, although she didn't seem to need them. She had what she had always wanted, and was therefore more content with her lot in life than any of them.

Next day, with the raft checked over for any needed repairs and a good stock of food onboard, they relaunched it, climbed aboard, and set off down the river on the next stage of their journey.

When the wind was in a favourable position, they used the jacket sail method of gaining a little extra speed, but this time people were replaced with poles cut from the forest, and with Greg in charge of positioning the sail and a crude rudder made from poles they had lashed together, they made good progress.

They stopped each evening to replenish their supplies and sleep, but finding suitable places to land the raft was getting difficult as the forest was constantly changing.

At first it just came down to the water's edge, but as they went even further south, the trees seemed to invade the very waters they floated on, a massive tangle of roots reaching out for several hundred metres into the river.

More than once they had to spend the night on the raft, tying it to the gnarled tree roots so that it didn't drift away as they slept.

Because of the root tangle reaching out so far into the river, getting ashore to find food was becoming increasingly difficult, and one day Glyn announced that he thought they had reached the most southerly point they were likely to reach unless there was some other means of transport.

The sun was now nearly overhead at noon, and Arki agreed that this was a sign that they had gone as far south as was necessary to comply with the instructions in the back pack so long ago.

It was now just a matter of finding a suitable place to make a permanent camp, and then develop their skills to combat whatever they found which might threaten their survival.

They found one area which at first glance looked promising, at least for landing the raft.

A vast flat expanse of sand stretched inland, the forest fringing it in a curtain of dark green in the distance. As they drew near the beach, the radiation alarm screamed, so they beat a hasty retreat, Glyn having great difficulty in convincing the others that it was dangerous to land there.

It was now blatantly obvious that all the women were with child, and a permanent home site had to be found soon.

Despite the new growth the binding creepers of the raft were putting out enabling them to keep the whole thing together, the raft itself was becoming waterlogged and some of the timbers were beginning to break up, so they now had little option other than to make landfall as soon as possible.

Fresh food supplies from the forest were becoming more difficult to obtain, so what they were able to get was supplemented by fishing, which by now had developed into a fine art. The flat stones which Brendon had suggested they kept came in useful for making the fire on in order to cook the fish, there being little chance of the raft catching fire as the wood was now almost soggy underfoot.

At long last, a dark smudge on the horizon broke the monotony of the dark green forest which so densely fringed the river bank, not that they had seen the actual bank for a very long time now.

As they drew nearer, the dark smudge took on a more definite shape, and the hopes of a safe landing increased as a series of rocks reached out into the water towards them. At this point, the river was so wide that the opposite river bank couldn't be seen, and the feeling that they might be blown out into the ever expanding river by a vagrant wind added to their desire to set foot on terra firma again.

The raft rounded the promontory, hit a submerged rock, and the man standing at the front calling out directions toppled head first into the water. He came up spluttering and trying to spit out the water he had inadvertently swallowed. 'What ever you do, don't drink this stuff, it's foul,' he said as they hauled him aboard.

Arki knelt down to dip a finger into the water and tasted it. 'I know what this is, I read about it in one of the books. It's called a sea, a vast expanse of water which has salt in it. These seas can be huge, hundreds or even thousands of kilometres across, and all rivers run into them.

We must have come to the end of the river and this is the beginning of the sea. You can't drink it or you'll be ill, so don't try.'

On the other side of the line of rocks, a long stone slab ran from far up on the land to reach out into the sea beneath them. They turned the raft using the guiding poles, and as the sodden logs hit the sloping stone slab, several broke away, leaving them no option but to disembark for good.

'This isn't natural stone,' Arki announced, 'it's the same as the concrete building we were in during the storm, so that means it's man made. But just look at the size of it!' he exclaimed.

What it had been they couldn't even guess at, but they were glad it was there as it gave them a safe open landing place, clear of the ubiquitous forest.

Ten:
Actuality

THE SUPPLIES WERE carried ashore together with anything else they could salvage from the now fast disintegrating raft, and they headed up the concrete ramp to make camp.

The top of the ramp gave way to a sand and pebble area with the forest some several hundred metres distant, so Glyn took out the radiation detector and waved it about over the ground to make sure it was safe. There was the gentle tick, tick which indicated the normal background count, and so the area was pronounced fit to make camp on.

A foraging party set off across the sands for the forest, to return later laden with fruit and nuts much to everyone's delight. Meanwhile, Brendon had organized the building of a fire pit, a rectangular enclosure of rocks with a short column of carefully laid stones at each end to support a cooking pole.

Earlier that day they had caught a large fish, taking four of them to land it on the raft, and this was now skewered on a pole and left to sizzle over the hot coals of the fire.

That evening all agreed that it was the finest meal they had eaten since leaving the ship, and all they now needed was a local fresh water supply to complete their needs.

One of the men from the foraging party suggested that Glyn should come and see the trees in the forest, as they were unlike any that had been seen before. There were also some strange noises high in the canopy, but they couldn't see what was causing them.

Glyn agreed that such things should be investigated and a party would go out in the morning to see what mysteries the new forest held. The guards were posted for the night, and everyone retired for a well earned sleep, only being disturbed once by a shrill screech from the depths of the forest.

As the sun crept lazily up over the horizon, the first meal of the day was consumed, and then the exploration party set off excitedly for the forest to see what it held.

Arki had brought his long cutting blade, and four guards with pointed poles formed the protection squad, not that they would be able to protect very much if they came across anything like a land version of the creature which had nearly overturned their raft, but no one was thinking too seriously about that possibility.

The first barrier to their progress was a thick tangle of dark green bushes intertwined with a very tough creeper. There were signs of where the foraging party the previous night had forced their way in, but most of the growth had recovered.

'I think we should cut a way through this tangle, and when it's dry, burn it. That way we should achieve a permanent pathway through.' Glyn looked around for approval of his idea, but Arki had already begun hacking away with his blade. With Arki cutting and the others dragging the severed greenery out into the open to dry, it wasn't long before they had a wide clear pathway into the main forest.

'These are the trees I was telling you about,' said one of the men, 'what do you make of that?' pointing to a branch which had obviously come from one tree and was now joined into a different trunk as though it had grown out of it.

Looking around, they could see that all the main trees were of the same kind, sharing branches one with another, forming a huge grid system of immense strength against even the most severe of gales.

Dotted amongst the joined up monsters of the forest were smaller trees, some bearing fruits, nuts or flowers, but they all seemed to be separate, growing in whatever clearing they could find amid the huge matrix of the forest giants.

The further they went into the forest, the taller the trees became, until eventually Glyn deemed it too dangerous to go on as the massive canopy overhead blocked out most of the light, and there were no fruiting trees for them to harvest anyway. A couple of ear piercing shrieks from high up in the trees got everyone a little edgy, and a hasty retreat from that dark and threatening part the forest ensued.

When they returned to the blazing sun of the forest edge they were surprised to find the scrub they had cut and laid out to dry had shrunk to half its size and was ready for burning.

'I don't understand this,' said Glyn, 'we haven't been gone all that long, so how come all this greenery had dried out so soon?' It puzzled all of them for a while, until someone discovered that the structure of the plants was such that once the stem had been cut, the internal fluids drained away quickly to be absorbed by other nearby plants.

'Must be nature's way of conserving moisture in the forest.' Arki thought, as no other explanation seemed to fit.

After the midday break, the gang went out to the forest again, one of them carrying a blazing fire brand, and Glyn instructed the others to pull all the dried foliage back into the area they had cut it from in order to make sure that it didn't grow back again in a hurry.

Once the dried material was in place, the flaming brand was applied, and they all ran back from what was almost an explosion, as the dried plants rapidly burst into vivid red and yellow flames, searing some of the still growing plants on the side of the pathway.

Within minutes the fire had died down, and the ground was blackened and smooth where the fire had been, not a vestige of plant life remaining.

Someone came up with the idea of building shelters to protect the group from any possible rain storms, although the skies had been a clear blue for days and not a cloud in sight. Glyn thought it a good idea as it would give everyone something to do, and they just might need a shelter one day.

Several days later, and after much hard work, a small village of living huts and two store sheds had been constructed with materials from the forest, and a palisade built around them to keep out anything which might fancy the inmates for a light snack one dark night.

They gradually got used to the hideous noises which emanated from the forest during the hours of darkness, and although no one had seen any creatures, they were left in no doubt that they existed somewhere nearby.

The next two new arrivals took everyone by surprise, except the mothers, and even they were surprised by the seemingly short gestation period.

'There's something funny going on,' Glyn confided to Arki one day, 'these births seem to be coming along far too quickly, I'm sure it was never as quick as this on the ship.'

'Know what you mean, I can't explain it either, unless when on the ship we had a distorted sense of time. Maybe the ship needed to do that for some reason, although I can't think of one offhand.' Arki looked as puzzled as Glyn felt.

'Oh, and we'll have another problem before too long, and that's clothing. How can we make cloth? So far I haven't found anything from which to make the thread, let alone weave it. With all these children coming along, we'll have to think of something soon.' Glyn was beginning to feel that he couldn't provide the necessary items they were all used to, and it was his job as leader to do that.

'We'll think of something.' was all Arki could say.

The days raced by, more children were born, and the stockade reinforced after someone thought he saw an animal twice his size in the forest. Most made jokes about the mythical creature until they found several large clawed footprints near the stream from which they got their water, and then the stockade went up another metre or so, and armed guards fetched the water.

They were none too sure what part of the year they were in, but as the temperature kept going up a little each day, they assumed that full summer was approaching, and soon everyone was stripped to the waist.

A small boat made from a laboriously hollowed out fallen tree enabled them to go fishing in pairs, until one team returned with a tale of a super fish which nearly pulled them out to sea and then tipped the boat over, so they had to cut the lines in order to get free of it.

Glyn suggested another type of boat be made by lashing two boats together a couple of metres apart to give extra stability. Bigger fish were soon on the menu as the boat now held four people. A wide leafed plant on the edge of the forest provided the material for a usable sail, several leaves being stitched together with split creeper strands.

Everyone enjoyed the sailing trips in the cool of the evening until someone saw a very large fish like object circling their boat. They put the baited line overboard to see if they could catch it, and the first half metre of the boat disappeared between a vast set of flashing white teeth.

After that, it was only the fishermen who sailed the sea for quite some time, and then only in pairs of boats.

The hunt for some plant which would supply them with a material to manufacture thread went on, but nothing was found which was soft enough to be made into cloth.

So far, no one had fallen prey to the creatures of the sea or the forest, but there had been a few near misses, and Glyn gave those unfortunates a fairly vitriolic tongue lashing to drive home the point that vigilance was of paramount importance at all times. With their present numbers, they couldn't afford to lose anyone.

By what they thought was the approach of autumn, the last of the women had given birth and those who had produced the first children were well and truly pregnant again, including Mia, who was heading the field.

Glyn impressed on all that it was their duty to teach the children all they could remember from the ship days, as there were no books or other means of keeping a record of what had happened. The writing materials in the backpacks didn't last long, and although they could be cleaned off and written on again, there was a limit as to how many times this could be done, and it was doubtful if the flimsy material would stand the test of time anyway, as far as permanent records were concerned.

Winter was hardly winter, it just got a little cooler in the evenings, and then they were into spring again, which was the point at which the great adventure had begun when they were forced to leave the ship, or was it? No one was sure, and few cared.

Glyn and Arki worked incessantly to make sure that everyone had a skill which contributed to the overall good of the group, and where possible, two skills were encouraged.

The occasional new item of food was added to their menu, and a large area of forest had been cleared using fire, the idea being to plant fruit bearing trees close to the compound, just in case something unpleasant was found in the forest and it curtailed their foraging until it could be handled.

The months went by, the seasons, such as they were, came and went, and the group steadily grew in numbers.

Glyn was still obsessed by what he considered to be a very rapid gestation period, and this was further compounded when he realized that the children were growing up at an apparently accelerated rate as well. Arki couldn't or wouldn't shed any light on the subject, although he had his own ideas on the matter.

As there had been no overt attacks from sea monsters for some time, an expedition set off to go along the coastal waters to see what else there might be a little further away.

They returned in due course with two new fruits and cuttings from the plants which had produced them, safely tucked away in a bed of damp moss and ready for propagation in the new cleared area at the back of the compound.

Although they were not strictly farmers, everyone grew something, and most had a skill which produced goods other members of the group needed.

By the time of the third round of births, the first was well developed and mimicking most things their parents were doing, apart from reproducing, as yet.

Mia's third child was a girl, and it was then that the normally hard nosed Glyn melted a little, and became a great favourite among the children of the group.

He had wondrous tales to tell, most containing a nugget of information which would aid their survival in later years. He was still hell bent on education, in one form or another.

One expedition brought back several pieces of the shiny metal, which after being tested by Glyn's radiation device, were seized upon by Arki whose cutting blade was getting thinner by the day, and new blades were fashioned complete with sturdy handles and a scabbard for protection.

A few more years went by, and the first generation were ready for partnering off to produce young of their own.

'I wish I knew how the medic worked out the pairing for spreading the genes correctly.' Glyn said to Arki one day.

'Shouldn't worry, if I were you,' Arki replied, somewhat disinterested in the subject, 'there's enough of us now for nature to sort it out. I think you should let the youngsters chose among themselves, as long as it's not between brother and sister.' And the matter was closed for the last time.

There were several deaths among the oldest of the group over the next year or so, and it drove home the point to Glyn and Arki that although they were not among the oldest, their time for departure was coming up.

The group was now too big for the comparatively small compound which had been their starting place, and an expedition along the coast had found another suitable site only a few kilometres away which could easily take half the group to begin a new colony.

Glyn decided that it would be best for all if Arki took charge of the new group, and established it on the newly found site along the coast.

They would split the people down the middle on a voluntary basis, so that each group would have an equal mixture of young and old, and so it was done.

After the split, Glyn missed Arki more than he ever thought he would. There was no one else quite like him, no one else would stand up to his more outrageous ideas, and no one else had the ability to dust him off and stand him on his feet after taking a mental tumble.

Over the years, they did meet, taking it in turns to visit each other's compounds and exchanging ideas, but it wasn't quite the same again, and Glyn missed his old friend deeply.

It wasn't that long before both groups needed to split again, and new clearings in the forest had been prepared and shelters erected in anticipation of the event.

Glyn now had to be carried around in a wicker chair on two poles, and it irked him terribly. He and Mia had produced fourteen children, the youngest five now having children of their own and just as keen as their father to make their mark on the world.

He still couldn't reconcile the fact that gestation and the growing up process of the children took so little time, and as he didn't have anyone to argue with now, he had to keep his thoughts to himself.

One thing he did do was to keep a record of the average heights of the children when fully grown, and the data he had accumulated caused him even more concern. Each generation was a little shorter and stockier than the previous one, but as the difference was only small from one generation to the next, it didn't become apparent to the others.

Great efforts had been made to discover some means of making cloth, but there didn't seem to be a plant with the right kind of fibres anywhere in the forest.

Some plants produced fibres which made very strong cords and ropes, but they were too course for fabrics, as the prospective wearers very soon found out.

Eventually the old clothes wore out, but by then everyone had got used to roaming about as naked as the day they were born, only the most elderly clinging to the remnants of the old fabrics to cover their dignity and anything they considered shouldn't be on public view.

A few years on, and he was very frail indeed, and had to be waited on for all his needs. Just before his demise, Glyn sent a message to Arki about his latest discovery.

Using help from many eager hands, but keeping the information gathered thereby to himself, he had found that not only were the generations getting shorter each time, but they were also growing a little more body hair. It was very fine and toned in well with their golden brown sunburn, but it was there nevertheless.

Glyn died in his sleep one night, a contented smile on his face as if he had solved some great mystery, sadly it was before the message came back from an equally aged Arki that he had noticed the same thing.

The human population of earth was taking off again, the groups splitting and penetrating further into the forest, while some preferred to stay close to the coastline.

Without Glyn and Arki banging the education drum, as it were, the urge to educate the young had weakened more than somewhat, and the recipients of such teaching as there were, found it difficult to relate the little their parents taught them to the facts of surviving in the forest.

Forest lore went down well, was easily understood and could be applied to life. If you got it wrong, you usually didn't get a second chance. Spaceships which weren't what they seemed to be, and stories of an old earth long gone by were irrelevant, and didn't stay in the memory for very long, and so the old tales died out, except for a very few persons who did seem to enjoy them.

The creatures of the forest hadn't been exactly standing still while all this was going on, and some very strange and unpleasant ones had wandered in from afar, seeking a better environment or a new supply of food.

Unfortunately, some particularly nasty ones moved into the vicinity of one of the new groups, and they were ill equipped to deal with the new threat.

A frantic messenger broke into the old base camp early one morning with the news, and a veritable army of knife and spear carriers set forth at great speed to even up the odds a little, which they did admirably.

It was a pity that the creatures of the forest didn't have the gift of speech, for if the story of the massacre had gone the rounds, they wouldn't have troubled the humans again, but they didn't, and they did, if you see what I mean.

As the years rolled by, the new generations had to move further into the forest, but this posed a problem.

The deeper into the forest they went, the darker it got at ground level, so there was a natural limit to the degree of penetration that was viable, until some bright spark suggested an alternative, that they move up into the levels just below the canopy.

The trees deeper in the forest were truly giants, and the massive branches which linked each tree to its neighbour made a very efficient highway for the new forest dwellers to travel on. Any threatening predators were quickly despatched and each new enclave kept in communication with its neighbours via the linking branches.

They didn't have it all their own way. The forest was developing its own brand of life forms, and these migrated hither and thither as space and food supplies dictated, and occasionally there were clashes and casualties on both sides, but usually the humans won.

As each new generation matured, and the strongest members took up the senior positions in each group, the racial memory of their beginnings began to fade as survival necessities became of prime importance, only a few dedicated people passed on the old stories down to the next generation, and that was only to those who were interested.

The metal cutting blades so painstakingly wrought by Arki so long ago, began to wear out and eventually became useless, odd pieces of metal were found but the method of converting them into useful devices was long forgotten, and the finds became objects of mysticism, adding to the tales told by the elderly of bygone ages to entertain the young or anyone else who would listen.

The radiation detector lasted for a very long time, but what it detected and the significance of its signals were forgotten long before the solar powered regeneration and power storage system failed, which was a pity, as several groups wandered into areas of high radiation and subsequently suffered massive radiation burns and genetic damage, which led to their demise.

Any form of clothing had been discarded long ago, as the temperate climate suited the unclad figure, and was less restrictive of movement.

A few artefacts survived and were added to by finds from the old ruins of the pre destruction period, but their uses were beyond the comprehension of those who found them, and generally they were relegated to the safe keeping of the Story Tellers, which most groups seemed to have acquired.

The Story Tellers performed a useful service to the groups, as they studied the use of herbs and other useful gifts of the forest for the treatment of ailments and accidents, worked out methods of combating the more deadly invaders of a group's area, and generally kept an eye on the mores of their enclaves.

The forest grew and gradually took over most of the land masses, new species appeared from time to time adding to the continual diversity of life on Earth, and a kind of stability was achieved.

Nature, for want of a better word, rested for a while, allowing her new creations to find their own niches in the rich panoply of life which now pervaded the shattered remains of what so-called civilized man had wrought upon the Earth, and although it would never be the same as before, it was surviving well, despite the differences.

As always, she would take her time before the next great thrust forward to populate the universe with sentient beings, whatever form they might take.

But generally speaking, those which survived the best seemed to be equipped with two arms, two legs, a trunk and a head, although what went on in the head was not always as predictable or reasonable as she might have hoped for.

Nature had one invaluable thing in her favour, time, and there was plenty of that.

THE END

**More from sci-fi-cafe.com
by David Reynolds-Moreton**